# DANCE MOVES
## OF THE
## NEAR FUTURE

# DANCE MOVES
# OF THE
# NEAR FUTURE

# TIM CONLEY

New Star Books | Vancouver | 2015

NEW STAR BOOKS LTD.
107 - 3477 Commercial Street | Vancouver, BC V5N 4E8 CANADA
1574 Gulf Road, #1517 | Point Roberts, WA 98281 USA

The publisher acknowledges the financial support of the Canada Council for the Arts, the Government of Canada through the Canada Book Fund, the British Columbia Arts Council, and the Province of British Columbia through the Book Publishing Tax Credit.

Cataloguing information for this book is available from Library and Archives Canada, www.collectionscanada.gc.ca.

ISBN: 978-1-55420-097-9
Also available as an ebook in epub and mobi formats:
ISBN (epub): 978-1-55420-105-1
ISBN (mobi): 978-1-55420-106-8

Cover and book design by Oliver McPartlin
Printed on 100% post-consumer recycled paper
Printed and bound in Canada by Imprimerie Gauvin, Gatineau, QC
First printing, May 2015

for Neil Hobkirk

# CONTENTS

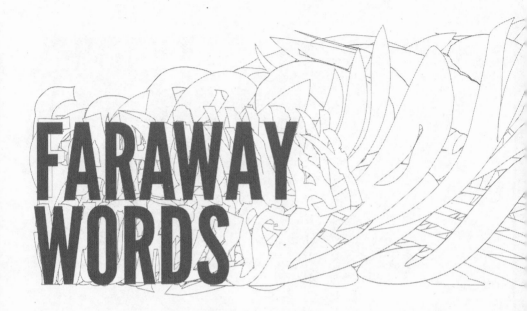

# FARAWAY WORDS

Now the evening may have been pleasant – at least the winds were no longer screeching – but the feeling of impending rain in the air is all I really remember about it. And I must have zigzagged quite a distance, for my sore feet were complaining. Only when I could walk no further did I literally come across the inn. The concierge, the kind of person who actually claps her hands when excited, was beside herself. Welcome, welcome, you look exhausted, such a long trip, you'll need rest to enjoy yourself, so much for you to do and see here, especially on your first visit, you won't be disturbed here, if there's anything you need. And, finally, Enjoy your stay. Perhaps I did not look as wretched as I felt. In any case, I passed by her and made for my room, knowing that there would be no reading before bed this night.

Darkness received me inside, and I let my clothes fall to the floor as I made my way, with some little bumps from corners and upholstery to my fatigued, uncaring body, to the bed. There I sprawled. Instead

of muttering over the day's events, my thoughts were absorbed in an
unexpected memory of another occasion of travel and exhaustion. My
brother and his lover Teresa and I hiked many miles one spring day, with
a picnic lunch and much bright laughter between us. This was a birthday
wish of his, this jaunt, and by the sun's bleeding we were none of us
able to stand. One sour moment came back to me then, as I lay in some
wild shape on the cheap bedding, the first discordant note from this
happy pair that had ever come to my ears. My brother had stumbled,
nothing damaged, but had to extract a pebble or some other irritant and
reached out to grasp Teresa's forearm to steady himself as he bent down.
Unaware or startled, she moved her arm, and crash went my brother,
down again, this time further down the incline and badly bruised in the
end. The comedy that should have been there wasn't, and the private
sounds of bickering, no matter how low, can always be perceived by and
make uncomfortable a witness like myself. Trying to keep enough paces
behind them for the moments of cooling, I nevertheless saw Teresa's

features make some infinitesimal change that I cannot even now characterize. She was going to speak, perhaps, but decided against it – but no,
wait, I thought then that she did say something, or made an unexpected
sound, a slippery *hiss* –

This impossibility startled me onto my elbows and there, an
arm-and-a-half's length from me, was the source of this nasty sound.
Never in my life have I seen such a thing, never before had I been so
terrified. A devil in the darkness! To be jolted awake by the toothy
hiss of this squat monster at the end of the bed, its eyes bending
and its haunches raised, is not something I would wish on my worst
enemies. My slowly reaching for and turning on the lamp earned
another hiss and greater tensing of its dwarfish form and seeing
it more clearly in the light did not reduce my fear. It had tiny but
dangerous-looking claws and bared teeth and a bizarre sort of mask-
like ribbon of black hair or fur around its eyes, which were cruelly
opaque marbles. Twitching behind it was a black-striped tail which
billowed out and came to a point.

How long did we contemplate one another, my ferocious
bedmate and I? Neither of us budged, and I knew not what to think,
never mind to register how many seconds or minutes were passing.
There was a scream in my throat looking for an exit, a man running
through a hallway of doors trying this one and then that, each
one revealing a brick wall. If not a brick wall then the eyes of this
horror at the foot of the bed. At last, the creature's head lowered an
inch and its nostrils quivered. It made a decision – either I was no
threat or, perhaps, inedible – and backed away. With odd dexterity it
lowered itself down the side of the mattress and calmly went off to
attend to whatever unimaginable business it had in mind elsewhere.

When I judged it to be at a safe distance, I leapt across to the
door and, once in the hallway, finally released the scream. It died out
with my breath just as I reached the front desk and the immovable
object, the concierge. She began to welcome me to the inn, such a
long trip and you're sure to enjoy the hospitality here, but I cut her
off: There's an unspeakable monster in my room!

4

She blinked emphatically a number of times and was forced to listen to my account of my waking shock, of the standoff, of my escape. As soon as I uttered the word *barely*, however, my alarm subsided for I remembered I was entirely naked, and my speech ended with something like an undignified whimper.

Oh! The concierge's look of distress dissolved and gave rise to one of embarrassed amusement. You must have gone into my apartment by mistake and startled my parrot.

I have never seen a parrot before, I said cautiously, and thought to myself, and doubt I have tonight.

He's a bit on the precious side. High-strung, you might say.

Determined to be polite and stay on the good side of my hostess, though equally intent on retaining the moral high ground of one who has the right to complain, I said, That may be so, but I was always under the impression that parrots were . . . without teeth.

Her immediate answer was a chuckle. Forgive me, sir, she said, but you've been reading too many fables and are misinformed. My parrot is a very good bird and I doubt he meant you any harm. He was very probably just as startled as you were. Let us go back and retrieve your vestments from my apartment.

I'm not going back in there with that beast, I said firmly.

I will go in myself, if you tell me where you put your things, and you can stand outside the door. Then we will secure you in your own room. Does that sound satisfactory?

Yes, I replied, but I must tell you that I have serious doubts about your parrot's claim to be a parrot. In some encyclopædia or another I have glimpsed a picture of that genus of bird, and that image and the fanged terror that is in your apartment do not correspond.

But the concierge did not appear to be listening and had already turned down the hall with a ring of keys in hand. I followed and heard her say, I hope he's not too riled up. He can really jabber on sometimes when he's upset.

She looked back at me when I expressed amazement that the

animal could do this. Did she really mean that it could speak? Her expression told me that she felt her sense of humour was perhaps now being tested, though assuredly (her expression went on to observe) to no avail. Parrots, she explained, have the ability to speak words and phrases. Your encyclopaedia must be worthless if it did not tell you that.

Before I could protest that I did understand that parrots could speak, she was at the door and let herself in while making some cooing sounds for the animal within.

I don't know how long I stood there but then one always says that sort of thing when one is not conscious of doing anything in particular, and perhaps especially when naked in a hotel corridor and half-scared to death. When in fact it occurred to me that I had no idea how long I had been standing there, I devised a means of occupying this time with stylized measurement of its passing. This amounted to counting, almost aloud, the number of days since my brother and I had last spoken with one another: six hundred and ten, six hundred and eleven, six hundred and twelve; like counting the hours he had been gone ahead that morning, then that afternoon, leaving me alone with her; and perhaps six hundred and thirteen, now, for what time of night was it?

The concierge returned and, taking in one last none-too-sur-reptitious survey of my nudity, handed me my clothing. Turning her back, which I did not immediately recognize as a cue to get dressed, she began talking once again of how good it was to have me as a guest and about what a good time I was sure to have during my visit.

Yes, I finally answered, clothed again.

She turned, beamed, and gestured towards the door to her room. Now, she said.

Now?

You really don't know anything about birds, do you? They can be very high-strung. Mine in particular is a little on the precious side. Any calamity will disturb them, set them jabbering for days and, what is worse, most of it is incoherent. You cannot imagine how it is to have to cohabitate with a fretting parrot.

No, I said, and after a pause said again, No.

The only thing for it is an apology, she said. Nothing fancy, but then again don't lay on with any unnecessary irony. They can detect insincerity. They're very alert birds.

Her open palm was still aimed at the door.

You did give him quite a scare, she added.

I! I cried, but could think of nothing more to say. The unruffled geniality of the concierge was like an irresistible prod, and though the last thing I really wanted to do was to encounter again the beast in that room, I found myself walking through the door as it was opened for me. My eyes may even have been closed – everything happened with a pace so seemingly determined by some unheard music. I was its deaf dancer, or a senseless marionette.

My eyes must have been open now, for the deep red light of the room permeated every point in sight except the recognizable squat form that sat on the mattress. It returned my stare but made no motion and seemed entirely undistressed by my reappearance. The black mask lent its gaze a bizarre kind of authority, the way spectacles sometimes do to otherwise undignified faces. Its confidence was not infectious, however, and it was with a tremulous, frightened, and rushed whisper that I at last spoke:

For my unexpected entry earlier and for disturbing you I am truly very sorry.

I coughed, and repeated the last word again, while my squirming hand, the first part of the body to turn coward, retreated behind me to touch the door, and one foot dug in at the toe's pivot to join in the escape. Then the rich, deep voice of the beast rose out of the red:

The word *apology* means, said the parrot, or can be said to mean, *faraway words*. Yet the sovereignty of conscience tells us that no matter how many such words and gestures of apology are given, we never truly reach any distance between ourselves and what we have done. Our hope lies in the equal but distinct sovereignty of the imagination, which affirms that neither can we be sorry for, nor attain distance from, what we have not done.

Teeth sparkled from a ferocious, self-satisfied grin.

Like a reprimanded student, I hung my head, and then flung myself out of the room, pressing my back against the door once free of it. He's a decent sort, I babbled to the waiting concierge. Took it extremely well. No problem. Everything sorted out. Now I'm very tired and would like to retire now to my own room now, please.

She chuckled, not perhaps at anything I had said but at some remembered joke, then led me down a hallway I did not remember having ever been in before, to a door that bore my old number. I muttered thanks and went inside, and heard her say: My parrot was pleased to meet you.

This new room had no one in it but me, with nothing to say.

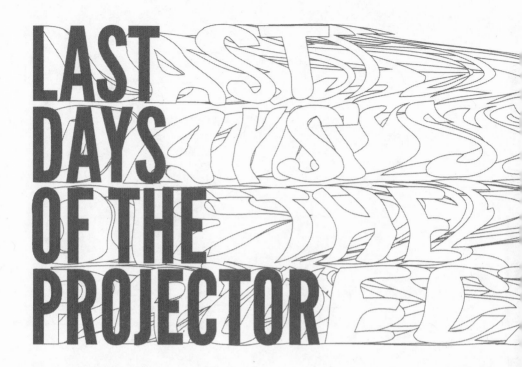

# LAST DAYS OF THE PROJECTOR

## 1

Where others have none, the cactus has a plan, has long had plans, for to be a cactus is not to be the lovers, who have each other, who can turn away from the future to face and caress each other with the feeling and daring and conviction of come what may, however utterly stupid or impractical or even doomed that turns out to be; nor is it to be the senator in his wheelchair since the fateful accident to which no one with a thought for his own welfare refers, for not only has the senator some undeniable degree of mobility despite what dark ways he may view it, but he has the power of capital and the altogether filial respect of the punchers and rustlers not to mention the veterans who served with him, and even his prejudices and stubbornness so sure to be his undoing do not prevent envy from sprouting in the most dispassionate beholder; nor is it to be the carpet, trod upon by generations but commanding respect, laden with symbols but more to the point itself a symbol, a symbol of many more values and

conflicts than even the absent-minded maid; yet come to that, too, to be a cactus, to be *this* cactus is not to be the maid, Fetchie, whis-tle-voiced and black and slow, comic for her meandering iterations and in turn pitiful for being comic in this way, as though her depic-tion was so openly dishonest as to make the injustice of it all right, and her own fate of little gravity but still, yes, so much weightier than that of the cactus; for, after all, come the hurricane or the raging brush fire or the Comanches, concern falls to the lovers, even if they do not look for it, and the senator, whose frailty must at last succeed his ferocity, and the carpet and Fetchie and the dogs and the framed photograph of mother and the sheet music of *Beautiful Dreamer* left untouched on the piano since she passed and the curtains blowing gently and the other dogs and the pinto and the pendant torn off in passion and hurled into the swimming hole and so on and indeed so on, the concern falling here and there like rain but not on the one thought undeserving or needless of rain, just as the cactus is without anyone to caress or command or be subjugated by, the cactus merits no concern. The cactus knows this and has given it a lot of thought. While Sid is trying to break in the new stallion and scrambling not to get trampled, the cactus, far from this foreground, is thinking and planning, and the cactus is planning when the army messenger arrives with the yellow moustache and the distressing news, when the sky breaks into an unnatural red and a myth of a chief's dying son is somewhat ironically invoked by a penitent observer, when the bloody straw settles at last after a long night's foaling.

2

It was autumn and my marriage was as gradually denuding itself of meaning as the trees their bright leaves. I had gone to catch a matinee for the sole purpose of getting out of the apartment. We had reached the point, my wife and I, where we no longer completed each other's sentences and thoughts not because we weren't aware of what they were but because we were too aware, too wearily aware, and attempts at surprise or deviation from a set course either simply failed, the pull of routine too strong, or failed to provoke more than irritation or sometimes pity for all concerned. We had no genuine differences of opinion but quibbled about menial things about which no opinion was seriously conceivable. When I tried listening to her, I heard all the more clearly how she was not listening to me, and I am certain that when she looked at me she found me unable or unwilling, perhaps one because of the other, to see her. I, who had little temper, would find myself shouting and the recognition that this behaviour was not, as I wanted to believe, characteristic yet was fast becoming chronic only helped to raise the volume and intensity of that shouting, while she oscillated between cold glares and fits of sobbing in locked rooms. On this particular occasion the door may or may not have been locked; I did not check; I went out, out anywhere, out to the streets and sooner or later into the movies.

3

"It was totally unreal," a man reported to a radio call-in show about the flood that had taken his hundred-year-old house apart the day before. He repeated this statement defiantly, argumentatively.


4

Difficult though it is to track down a copy, an old back issue of a now-defunct magazine for cinephiles includes an interview with the director, held many years after he had stopped making movies. The interview makes for disjointed reading, and the director, fairly old and at least a shade irascible at this point, seems reluctant to answer directly the questions put to him. Again and again he digresses, never to the point of incoherency, though never with a recapitulation or clear return to the ostensible subject at hand.

INTERVIEWER: Initial reviews of the film aren't much disposed to like it, but I noticed that nobody panned it outright. In fact, despite the various criticisms and complaints that they make, every one of them contains a kind of hesitation, as though there's *something* in the film nagging at them that prevents them from rejecting it, but none of them absolutely identifies what that *something* is. Did you notice that?

DIRECTOR: My mother had six fingers on each hand and though she took no special pains to conceal the fact almost nobody ever commented. Now was that because they saw and didn't want to be rude, or that they saw and so didn't know what to make of it that they couldn't even muster comment, rude or otherwise, or was it that they didn't see those six fingers at all? And I guess when I was young I asked her why she had six fingers and I had only five. Everybody liked to tell me that I asked that when I was young and at the time everybody in the room was holding their breath waiting for her answer. Unfortunately I don't remember what her answer was.

INTERVIEWER: The film's end is nothing if not cataclysmic, and that remains a big shock for audiences and critics alike.

DIRECTOR: Well, we had two camera guys, and they were dating the same girl. Pretty much everybody on the set knew about it but neither of them had quite figured it out. So naturally there would be jokes and when Eddie was staying for the night shoot for three straight nights, because we had to get some of those shots with just the right kind of sky and the right kind of wind and lighting and everything else, and also I remember we were having a few mechanical problems then . . . well, if Eddie was committed to those nights of shooting everybody knew that Gene was with the girl. And Eddie knew that Gene had a girl, and vice versa, but no clue between them about what all the coincidences pointed to. It was funny, that not knowing and all that knowing thick around it, like the water they say can be found inside the heart of a cactus, not that I ever checked that story for myself but if ever I'm stranded without a drop in the desert . . . Gene died, as you might know, in that big hotel fire about ten years ago. It would be a dreadful thing to be burned alive, don't you think?

5

You telephoned. It was a bad connection and you didn't say where you were calling from, and I was too discreet to ask (too foolish not to). You told me about a man you had watched on a train who was slowly, methodically pulling out his hair in long strands, with no sign of effort or alarm, but at a pace that was hypnotic, that effectively slowed the train, the movement of his eyes following the movements of his fingers withdrawing long strands of hair in strange, slow parallel with the movement of the passing world seen through the windows of the train. Rather than say or attempt to say how you felt, then or now, about what you were watching, you dwelt upon the details of those rhythmically conjoined movements and tried to imagine, with little enough success, what the man might have been thinking, watching himself come apart in this almost tender way, and no, I did not ask, how did you feel about what you were seeing, or even (though it might have been the same question, posed another way) why are you telling me this now, but instead asked only, what do you suppose he was thinking? You answered in a faraway voice: I can't be sure, but I suppose ... and your voice receded yet farther into an inarticulate sussuration, and I asked you to repeat what you had said, and called your name more than once, before hanging up, or to be more exact, before trying to hang up, for the receiver slipped from my hands in the act of cradling it, and I picked it up and put it again to my ear without thinking, and you were still not there, and then I did successfully hang up.

6

It's not exactly pointless to ask such questions as *how does a catastrophe take place* or *why should so-and-so alone survive*; these questions may even be inevitable, themselves the effect of catastrophe, the very definition of it: catastrophe is that which compels one to ask these questions. To do so is not *exactly* pointless, not without any possible point at all, but how much clearer everything would be were it truly so, for instead it is *more or less* pointless, pointless to a degree that cannot be determined. What makes asking these questions so excruciating is how one cannot understand precisely to what purpose one is thus compelled to ask them.

7

At first – it helps to treat the memory like a sequence of film – it was as though the flames were reverential, savouring the history of the place. It had been an office building for a law firm and a stationery supplier, briefly a flophouse, and now, in its last and longest incarnation, a cinema. The watching crowd's murmured exchange of these details of history was punctuated by gasps and cries that followed the bursting of windows, the fire inhaling the sky. One person said it was a shame, another asked if there was anybody inside, and a few minutes after nobody answered that question, someone else said it was a shame. The eyes of a child in a stained shirt were wide with unmistakable delight. Even over the whirrings of all of the digital cameras, the fire could be heard eagerly chewing away. The fire-fighters, none of them young, concentrated on saving neighbouring structures. The colour was so bright, so aggressive, that it could not help but suggest Technicolor. Most of the crowd stayed until the end, but then found that they had run out of things to say to one another, and returned to their less impressive because unburned homes.

8
A cactus does not actually have a heart. That is just a way of talking.

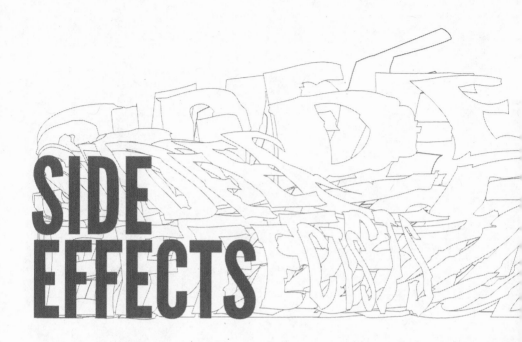

# SIDE EFFECTS

In the last August of my life, I went to a neurologist's office for some testing. A Christmas tree stood in the waiting room, which was furnished like a miniature and maybe even a parody of a middle-class living room. Resting snugly upon anodyne grey carpeting eerily incapable of generating the slightest static electricity were two facing patterned loveseats. In the framed print on the wall, a kitten seated before a glowing fireplace was looking up at the bigger, older cat beside it, very possibly its mother, whose translucency and lack of shadow behind vigorously indicated that it was a ghost, that it wasn't there in front of the fire the way the kitten was. I made a brief show of studying the picture from my seat so as to avoid having to enter into conversation with the sixty-something couple already waiting, seated together on one of the loveseats. That the kitten was looking at and thus could see the ghost cat but the ghost cat was placidly staring into the fire, not at the kitten, made me wonder whether the ghost cat was able to see the kitten.

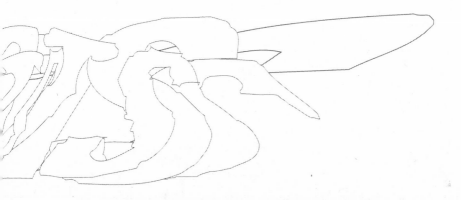

"Holding this thing," grumbled the husband.

"Set it on my purse," his wife said.

"I'll hold it," he said.

I looked searchingly at the ghost cat.

My name was eventually called by a short woman in a lab coat who waved me through a door from the waiting room into the interior offices, none of which resembled the waiting room at all. The bed in the room into which I was taken, however, was no hospital-special padded horizontal surface but a furniture store display, entirely alien within a room of otherwise unrelentingly typical clinic design: the off-white counter with anonymous drawers, the small sink and faucet, the blank boxes of unindividuated medical accessories, anything from sponges to hypodermics. The strangeness of this bed with the striped sheets and covers made its focal position almost distressing, like a lavish stage in a bare theater.

The lab-coated woman indicated that I was to sit down on

the bed as she rolled behind her a machine on a short dolly. In a cool but not unfriendly voice she told me to remove my watch and I asked her how long she had been a neurologist. She explained that she wasn't a neurologist but a technician while I removed my watch. She had been not a neurologist but a technician for six and a half years. Pointing to the machine, she said it was going to do most of the work for both of us, but I would have to lay down on the bed and she would have to record what the machine said on the clip-board under her arm.

Wiring the tips of two of my fingers and the side of my wrist to the machine, she explained that the doses of electricity from the machine were slight but sometimes produced some discomfort, though they had no side effects. I have always been curious about what exactly does and does not constitute a side effect, but it seemed the wrong time to ask, which struck me even then as an odd feeling since when could be a better time to ask such a question than when one is about to be exposed to whatever does or does not have side effects? That's me all over.

We chatted a little while she administered four or five funny little zaps, a mosquito pulling its punches. We talked about dogs, since she took care of stray dogs and I had been named after our family dog, and we talked about the poor design and governance of our city, since we both happened to deplore them.

"Many people don't like this part," she told me as she detached and then reapplied the sensors further up my inner arm, opposite my elbow.

"It hurts?"

"A more sensitive area."

This time the jolts bit more tightly and my forearm flailed. I tried not to take this personally.

"Maybe," I said, "many people don't like this test not because the shocks hurt, though they kind of do, but because the shocks make their arms jump around. People probably prefer to feel that their bodies move exclusively at their will."

She was then not looking at the equipment nor at the sheets on the clipboard she had been by stages filling with the relevant data about how my arms were jumping around, but at nothing at all, and I recognized this as an expression of her thinking about what I had said. At last she said, a little slowly, "You might have something there." Then, even more slowly, she said, "I believe that the world is full of echoes."

"Echoes?" (Had I heard her correctly? The jolts were distracting. I was suddenly thinking of my father, a man who lived to fix things, instructing me in my youth: "you have to respect electricity, for your own safety. It does what it's supposed to, but you have to respect it.")

"Is that a joke?"

"Is what a joke?"

So much for our connection, I thought in the silence that followed. I'd blown it, just like I had unintentionally blown it with Emma and with Charlene and with my cousin Lloyd and with the dentist's receptionist, missing what important matter was being said, was being offered, to me, and recognizing the missed opportunity too late. Zap, zap, zap; jump, jump, jump went my arm. Then we moved to my other arm and began again at the fingertips, and she suddenly resumed: "The world is full of echoes, like somewhere in the world just after this moment, maybe in a few minutes or a few hours, this same scene is going to be enacted again in just the same way, even with a technician who looks more or less like me and someone like you on a bed kind of like this one. Going through subroutines with variations."

We were now probing the area of the arm that most people do not (reportedly) like, and watching my arm flail as the other had, I could think of nothing in particular to say to this theory or intuition of hers. Then she said, "Hmm," and I asked what she meant by that.

"Your left's response is a little different from your right."

"Symmetry is overrated. Humans prefer things a bit askew,

don't you think?"

"Maybe," she said, but very affirmatively.

"So is this abnormal?"

"Not exactly. Okay, we're done here." She detached all of the wires and asked me to wait in the waiting room while she ran the results by the neurologist. This might take a few minutes, she explained, because she could only catch the neurologist between appointments. She adjusted an earring while looking over all that she had written on the clipboard.

"I understand the principle: the waiting room is for waiting."

"Yes," she said.

Back in the waiting room the wife was now alone, button-lipped on the loveseat, and another, slightly younger woman was standing by the window, looking out of it as though sternly willing whatever she was looking at to become more interesting to look at. I flipped through a magazine and read patches of an article on a youngish movie actor who had publicly announced that he would never make another movie. " 'The Hollywood machine can grind its wheels within wheels without me,' grins the boyish face with the wicked eyes." The article, disproportionately long for such a subject, was a continuous show of incomprehension, not so much at the ex-actor's decision, even despite the commercial success of most of his movies, as at the question of how he could possibly spend the rest of his life, a question not explicitly posed as such but lurking behind every paragraph.

Upon closing the magazine, vaguely wondering whether I had ever seen any of this former actor's work, I noticed my bare wrist, and quickly checked my pockets for my watch. The technician's head poked back into the waiting room at that moment. She advised me that everything "looks fine" and that I ought to make an appointment with my family doctor, to whom the test results would be sent the following day.

"Great," I said, "I think I left my watch in the, ah, testing room."

"You're sure it's not here in the waiting room?" she asked.

I shook my head but glanced back and found both of the women in the waiting room staring at me with mild but entirely unconcealed excitement. The wife on the loveseat suggested that the missing item might be under the loveseat opposite, a suggestion not only contrary to my memory but undercut by the simple fact that the possible hiding place was well within her own range of vision. To satisfy everyone, I bent down and looked, and then dramatically dug into my pockets again.

"Hmm," the technician said again, and led me back to the room with the bed in it that was not a bedroom. A man was now in the room, though he had not passed me from the waiting room. It was as though he had spontaneously materialized there in the short time I was gone and I could not guess whether he was the next patient to be tested or, who knows, the technician's husband off a little early from work, come by to pick her up. He looked nothing like me.

"The watch must be in here," I said, but couldn't see it.

"I didn't take it," he said, with an embarrassed laugh.

"No," I said. "I know. I must have left it here."

Eventually – I might as well cut to it because this is not the waiting room and you should not have to wait, though I did, while the bed was walked around, looked under, squinted at skeptically by all three of us – the watch was found. It was a watch of no great value, either monetary or sentimental, and could have been replaced without trouble. At one point in the search I even said as much and made to leave. "No," said the technician, who smiled at me. "We'll find it."

# THE RENAISSANCE

*War separated them. (2003–04)*

While Daniel was deployed in Afghanistan, Carolyn read a few books and had sex with a few men. From one of the books she learned that the second husband of Lucrezia Borgia was strangled when he was a mere nineteen years old. One of the men with whom Carolyn had sex, a bartender, had never heard of Lucrezia Borgia and evinced no apparent interest in the early sixteenth century. After they had sex – right after – he went and showered, and that left her with the feeling that he was cleaning her off of himself and so after the second time she decided not to have sex with him again.

Daniel's friend got two calls the day Daniel blew back into Toronto: one from Daniel, announcing the fact, and naming the restaurant where he would meet him, and one from a waitress at the restaurant, asking Daniel's friend to come to the restaurant because Daniel was there and he was acting really weird. Weird how? Quote like he's eating, you just have to come see unquote. So Daniel's friend

24

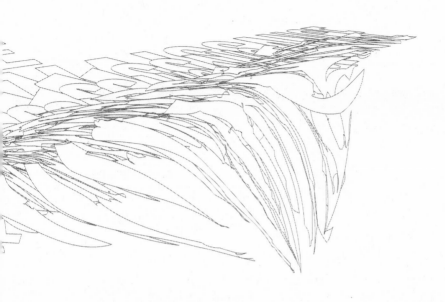

(who, incidentally, had never had sex with Carolyn, while Daniel was away or at any other time, but he had had sex once with the waitress in question, one of those friendly one-off situations with a friendly friend, and so she knew him sufficiently well to call him on this occasion) went to the restaurant and found Daniel with six or seven plates in front of him, penne and grilled shrimp and salad and more pasta and so on. He was on his fourth beer and it was not quite one in the afternoon. Daniel's friend ordered himself a burger, and Daniel said quote great idea, I'll have one of those, too, it's awesome to have real food again unquote.

Carolyn was at this time a graduate student in art history, though she had a hard time relating to other graduate students, even the couple of them that she had sex with. She disliked how they all liked to repeat the word quote problematic unquote. She felt that the twentieth-century art so many of them talked about was insignificant in the fullest sense of the word (Titian was then her favourite artist). She didn't care for the way most of them dressed. But for some reason she couldn't bring herself to voice her displeasure at these things, and would listen and stir her coffee or sip her pint. She suspected that none of them would have much of a shot at survival in the world of boardrooms.

*They married in Venice. (2005)*
Quote sharp eyes and bad tongues unquote is the phrase Carolyn picked up from Burckhardt. It was a joke about the Florentines, though, not the Venetians. She actually preferred Florence to Venice, but one of the charms about Venice was that it was sinking, doomed, and after she left it, there was always a chance that it might sink right after she had gone, and then it would not be there any longer; but she would have seen it.

Another friend of Daniel's, a former military guy but not one who had ever been to Afghanistan, invited him to a charity fund-raiser dinner. He asked Daniel if he could say a few words about his time in Afghanistan and include a salute to his fallen comrades, which was the sort of regular fare at these fundraiser dinners, and Daniel agreed. But when Daniel showed up he was so strung out – his friend didn't know what it was, but it was there in his eyes – that it looked very unlikely that he would be able to manage any sort of coherent public address. Daniel's friend tried to make light of the situation, took him aside and asked him if he had quote prepared a few words unquote, and at first Daniel didn't seem to know what he was talking about. The fallen comrades thing, he was reminded, and as he clued in he nodded fiercely. His eyes were even less right than before. Daniel's friend told him not to worry about it and asked another military guy at the dinner to make the speech.

Carolyn developed a theory that Tintoretto was poisoned, though she didn't refer to it as a theory but as a quote crazy idea unquote, and despite that phrase vehemently held to it. One of her professors agreed that it was a crazy idea, but ignored the implicit invitation to supervise her research. When he stepped out of his

26

office for a moment, she grabbed a few books from his shelves and tore random pages out of each and stuffed them into her bag. She came close to telling one of the other graduate students about it one night, after several drinks, but didn't. Instead she told another graduate student, a week later, after several drinks, and after having sex with him, and also told him about almost telling the other graduate student. After a while, he asked which books they were. She felt he was missing the point, so she decided not to have sex with him again.

*Daniel's drinking increased. (2007)*
Daniel's drinking increased. He was kicked twice out of the same posh club where he did not have full membership himself. The second time he threatened the driver of the cab that the club had called for him, and the police came. His guarantor, an old friend and full member of the club, stopped taking his calls after that.

*She had never been sure about marrying him in the first place. (2003)*
Just before Daniel left for Afghanistan an army buddy of his from out west was crashing at their apartment in Toronto. He stayed for another week after Daniel left, and he and Carolyn had sex with her pressed against the window, looking out over the snowy city. She wondered after that whether Daniel was coming back, whether he might die in Afghanistan, whether he knew about her having sex against the window with his buddy, whether having sex against the window looking out over the snowy city might not be the most free she'd ever felt, how being engaged to be married to someone stationed in Afghanistan did not feel very free.

Daniel, in Afghanistan, played more cards than he had ever played in his entire life. He was not very good at cards, especially at poker, but he tried to play with enthusiasm. He collected prayer rugs with the idea of delighting all of his friends back home with them. One of the men who sold him several rugs for virtually nothing told Daniel that there was a dark king at his shoulder. Daniel began to jokingly call the king of spades his lucky card, but his poker did not improve.

*Tintoretto was probably not poisoned. (1594)*
When Carolyn's father had a heart attack, she took the view, also held by her mother, that it had been caused by the stress of the ongoing lawsuits against him and the couple of mines that he owned in South America. (Technically, he was nominally the owner of two and sat on the board of directors of two others, but nobody in the family liked specific numbers.) He was known as something of a quote force of nature unquote in the world of boardrooms and both Carolyn and her mother said that men like that do not simply die. Carolyn's father did not die, but the lawsuits continued.

The following spring Daniel led a troop on a training exercise in which they were to conceal themselves in a designated wooded area, and maintain radio silence. The exercise was actually a rather high-profile test of a new satellite program, which was supposed to pinpoint these soldiers who were otherwise undetectable on the ground. The satellite program could not find any trace of Daniel's troop. The programmers were disturbed; the commanders became alarmed and dispatched more men to search the area. A few hours of searching turned up nothing, until one officer led a few men into the small town at the edge of the wood and went into a pub. Their entrance there was toasted with great laughter by Daniel and his troop, who were more or less thoroughly pissed and very proud of having concealed themselves so effectively. The officer who had found them detailed this response in his report, and that caused some trouble.

*In the very same church where Michelangelo's "Moses" sits, Giulio Clovio is buried. (1578)*
Carolyn's official dissertation began with Giulio Clovio and, after a few pages on this subject, went nowhere. The unofficial dissertation, which gathered much more steam, was worked on when Daniel

was away, chauffering some general or other around. It had not only many more pages but also many more footnotes than the unofficial dissertation, and it was a complex argument about the poisoning of Tintoretto. She was not sure why she was writing it, but kept at it all the same.

No one in the military knew just what to do with Daniel at that point, and it was thought that making him work for this hardass general with no sense of humour would at least keep him out of trouble for a while. Daniel typically mistook this for an honour and liked to hint to the girls he met that owing to his being in the general's confidence he was privy to a good deal of top-secret information, quote high-level stuff unquote, including (if he were forced to give an example) a new satellite program that was able to precisely pinpoint soldiers who were otherwise undetectable on the ground. One girl who decided that this was impressive enough to warrant having sex with him had sex with him in a hotel. Unfortunately she answered the phone when Carolyn called the next morning, and that caused some trouble.

*Her father had a second heart attack. (2009)*
More people called him a quote force of nature unquote but the doctor did not. Daniel asked a lot of questions of the doctor, not all of them relevant. He was unable to let his gaze settle, and shuffled his feet.

One night Carolyn called up an old friend from her undergraduate days, a guy she had had a brief fling with, and met him for drinks. Just after the second round he caught on that she was inviting him to have sex with her in a hotel. He told her he was seeing someone and it was serious, and she icily told him that he was quote still incapable of understanding a single fucking thing unquote and left him to pay the bill while she walked out into the night alone.

*Daniel's drinking increased. (2008–09)*
We have already covered this.

*It is not altogether impossible that Tintoretto was poisoned. (1594)*
The unofficial dissertation was well over four hundred pages by
Christmas, while the official dissertation remained where it had been.
The unofficial dissertation was expanding in its conceptual scope, too,
and that Christmas while Daniel was escorting the hardass general
to some military conference out west, she began a new chapter on
the life and marriages of Lucrezia Borgia, with reference to the
advent of painterly perspective, the problem of self-fashioning, and
popular methods of uxoricide. Even her father's third heart attack on
Christmas morning did not slow Carolyn's progress, and by the next
day she hit the six-hundred-page mark.

Later that same day, Daniel placed an incoherent telephone
call to a friend in Toronto (not the one who had once had sex with
Carolyn, but the one who had once had sex with the waitress who
had been disturbed by Daniel's eating when he first returned from
Afghanistan). The friend asked quote are you all right unquote three
times during the conversation but could not make out what Daniel
was saying, though there was a kind of effort at emphasis in what
Daniel was saying. It was impossible to say whether this was because
the connection was bad or because Daniel was slurring his words or
muttering or yelling.

*The current situation. (2010)*
Man is still the measure of all things. (An unexpected – but, in
relative historical terms, brief – network failure occurred.) Daniel has
apparently not returned from Alberta, though the hardass general
was seen in Boston in early March. Carolyn has talked informally
and once formally with legal advisors about the possibilities of
divorce. Her unofficial dissertation has not yet been located. Its loca-
tion, and whether it was ever completed, she seems never to have
told anyone.

# SAVING THE WORLD

There were two shifts at the clinic, a day shift and a night shift.

On the day shift were Grace and Reggie and Olympia. Grace had worked there the longest but never made mention of the fact; she was known for never having a hard word for anybody. She was always asking after the patients' families, always remembered the name of every child and grandchild, and Reggie often joked about her perfect memory in that way of his. Olympia was the quietest of the three but she had the most energy, had to be told when to take a break.

On the night shift was an amorphous, gelatinous-looking blob that could raise itself to the ceiling or slink through the lowest crevice. It did not have a name.

Word came down, not altogether directly, from the City Health Office: in recognizing the surplus of clinics within the municipality, and in the interests of tightening the fiscal belts (just like everybody else had to), the clinic would be closing in three months.

"I've been coming here for my pills for twenty-six, no, twenty-seven years," said Mrs. Underwood in a voice neither exactly angry nor exactly sad, and had a quiet but fatal coronary right in front of a horrified Reggie, who had to be sent home for a few days.

I was the only one who consoled the blob, if consolation it may be called. Some years ago (though not nearly as long as Mrs. Underwood had been coming for her pills), it had enslaved my mind and I was utterly at its bidding on any night it chose. The phone would ring, I would answer, there would be no one on the other line, and I would know.

With two months to go before the closure, Olympia had a breakdown. At first she fell into an even deeper silence than usual, to the point that even recalcitrant folks tried cajoling her, but ultimately she exploded with a low howling. For over an hour she sat shaking in a chair dragged into the broom closet for the purpose, and the sound of her shook everyone. "Poor girl, this job may be all she has," said Grace.

The doors to the Director's house were locked but the windows weren't. It is hard to say which one of us found the other first. "Are you sure that's a real gun?" he asked. "There's a sure way to make sure," I answered, precisely as the nocturnal blob had instructed.

After the news broke the next day, it was all Reggie could talk about. He tried to insinuate that Grace was probably the kidnapper: it was obvious that she was a criminal mastermind, nobody ought to cross her, only the first step in a scheme. The investigating officers both told him not to make light of the matter.

The motel room in which the trussed Director of the City Health Office spent the next six days and nights was dingy enough to set a definite mood. I only left him to get food or, a couple of times, to meet up with the blob at the clinic. I noticed the usually translucent pink surface of my mind's master was clouding, greying, perhaps the result of stress. The Director declined to negotiate. "Just say you've reconsidered the distribution of health services, or recalculated the budget," I soothingly suggested. "Never," he answered.

There was less than a week left before the clinic's last day. Olympia emitted sudden but short howls from time to time and avoided extended discussions of any kind. When Grace inquired how Olympia's mother was doing, shrieking laughter came as the reply. "There's nothing funny about your mother," Reggie remarked, and altogether accidentally admitted that he had been having a semi-torrid affair with Olympia's mother for nearly a year. Grace slapped him, aiming for the face but hitting his left ear with her wedding ring, drawing blood.

The Director said he was getting tired of fast food. "I have a delicately poised digestive system," he said. "Everybody says so." Because I had no holidays owed me, I figured by now my job at the air control tower was probably gone. There was this game we used to play with newbies: we'd all talk about this plane that wasn't there, we'd have worked out its ID and flight plan beforehand and of course totally freak out the newbie. "But one time," I told the

Director, "there was this new guy in the tower named Zachary, and when we pulled this one on Zachary, he didn't freak out at all but instead called out that he had it, meaning he had it on his system and was going to guide this nonexistent plane from Bolivia or Madagascar or somewhere. Zachary was certainly one of the strangest guys I've ever met." After a few bites of hours-old burrito, the Director asked me what happened. I didn't understand. "What happened to Zachary?" the Director wanted to know.

Grace did not return to the clinic. She and her husband put their house up for sale the day before the clinic was to close, the same day that Reggie told Olympia that he had broken off with her mother and sincerely hoped that they might remain friends. A man dressed in pyjamas and a raincoat spoiled the moment by trying to shoplift thirty bottles of cough syrup.

The blob summoned me just before midnight. It was grey and mottled, stiffer in its movements. I began to cry, perhaps fearful of freedom, but was rebuffed: I was to build an exact replica of the clinic, as quickly as possible but without skimping a jot on accuracy, on the far outskirts of the city, behind the dump. The fruitlessness of the endeavour obvious to me, I agreed, and I think I would have agreed even if I could have resisted.

# THERE'S NO SUCH THING AS BACKGROUND MUS

Every now and again, Father would play the piano. There was almost no telling when he would choose to play, if he chose to play, but once the ritual began, every ceremonial step inexorably followed the next and no one in the house could be unaware that Father was about to play the piano. His washing of his hands, for example, in such heat and at such length that the pipes creaked; or his disconnecting of the two telephones, which involved tramping up and down stairs with a particularly determined step; or simply his silence, the silence of the house, sustained just long enough that everyone in the house might notice the silence and wonder what Father might be up to, a silence immediately prior to all of the other preparations: all pointed to his being about to play the piano.

There was, in those years, no way to speak of his playing. Once, a cousin who had stayed for a summer remarked at dinner during the last week of her visit that his playing was – these were her words – very pleasant, and when he looked up from his plate and

36

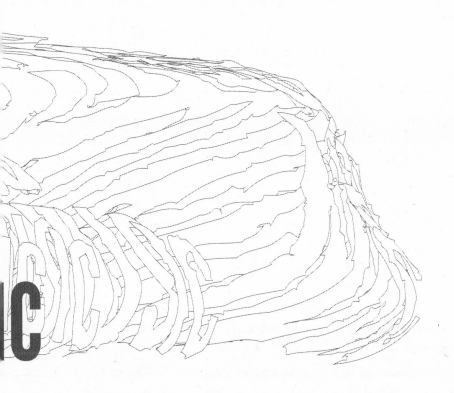

said nothing, she added words to the effect of how evident was his improvement as a player. Nobody ventured to add to that remark, not even Ingrid, probably in large part because it was not even close to true, and Father stared at her, this fond-faced cousin, as though she had, as Ingrid much later remarked, spoken in an incomprehensibly foreign language. He neither stopped staring nor resumed his rigid eating of his meal until after some time overtures toward a new subject of conversation were well under way.

No, it was not true: Father played as he always did, which is to say, haltingly, inevitably returning to the beginning of a piece if his progress through it seemed too cluttered with mistakes or if the pacing became hopelessly erratic. At least, those appeared to be his criteria. It was impossible to be sure, not simply because there were always mistakes and uneven pacing, somehow audible from every room in the house, but also because no one except perhaps Father himself recognized what piece he was working at, again and again.

Ingrid eventually suggested – again, much later, years later – that he was in fact composing, that he was playing some music he either indefinitely heard in his mind or was effectively making up as he went along. As evidence to support this hypothesis, she pointed to the scarcity of sheet music in the house and the fact that none of the mostly sentimental songs found among these sheets sounded at all like anything anyone could remember him playing. There was also the curious fact that Father very seldom listened to music himself, never spoke of it except in general reference to the soothing effect it had, and then only in the course of conversation, usually outside of the house.

These few lapses – if they might be called that – into discussion of music were keenly observed by anyone in the house who chanced to be present when they occurred, but certainly Ingrid was most especially attentive after her enrolment at the Institute, the tuition for which was paid, naturally, by Father. When an acquaintance of his, say, remarked on a concert he had recently attended, or made a passing reference to a certain song, or asked after Ingrid's ongoing studies at the Institute, Father might nod or acknowledge, with a slight bow of the head, that music had a soothing effect. If this acquaintance were to press further and, say, ask Father's opinion of Brahms, the reply would be the same: yes, indeed, music has soothing effects.

No one could remember when the piano had first come into the house. Both the piano and the house were very old. The piano-tuner, a creaking stick of a man, repeatedly remarked on how old the piano was, which was a kind of complaint he would always temper, perhaps to placate Father, with a vague comparison to the aging of fine wine. The piano-tuner, whose name no one could remember ever having heard, visited the house on no fixed or predictable schedule, or at least none that anyone except perhaps Father could discern. That piano of yours, he called it, no matter to whom in the house he might be speaking; that piano of yours is too old by half, that piano of yours will outlive us all, that piano of yours.

Just over a year after she began studying at the Institute, Ingrid had three scenes, as they came to be known, and the first of these involved the piano-tuner, who appeared one morning at the house when Father was absent on some errand or other. As usual, he asked to be taken to the patient and, as usual laughed, but of course he knew exactly where the piano was, the place from where it had never, so far as anyone in the house knew, been moved, the spot to which it seemed rooted. The piano-tuner liked to be led to the piano, if only out of politeness, or if only to insure that someone would be with him when he declared the piano old, someone to whom he could say, that piano of yours. That morning he happened to ask Ingrid, whom he found placidly watering plants in the kitchen, to lead him to the patient.

Ingrid abruptly broke into sobs, into helpless weeping, and clutched at the piano-tuner's long fingers, which he gently tried to pull away. Her voice went from shrill to hoarse as she asked him, implored him to take it away. Take what away, the piano-tuner gawped and gulped. No sooner had he freed his hands than she was on the floor, sniffling into his socks, crying out, take it away, over and over again, take it away, take it away, until two of her brothers eased her to her feet and took her trembling and blubbering from the room.

After this episode, this first of her scenes, Ingrid was more often away from the house. Though of course she could be counted on to be at the dinner table on time with everyone else – an empty chair at dinner, it was generally believed, would unnecessarily vex Father – she cited the need to practice and went out with her violin under her arm whenever she could. She also adopted a sterner demeanor, and when some months later she and the piano-tuner happened to meet each other as she was going out and he was coming in, she surveyed him with such coolness that he entirely forgot that day to refer to the piano as the patient.

Ingrid was studying both the violin and the flute, but the former was her greater love. Neither, however, was ever heard in the house. To any question about the progress of her studies, she provided only the most general answer, and none expressed any dissatisfaction with that, least of all Father, who seemed pleased enough, for all one could tell, to hear about the subject in this way, allowing others to make the inquiries while he almost imperceptibly nodded. No one else in the house had shown – or ever would show – any such interest in music, but it was impossible to judge whether Father was, as they say, quietly proud of Ingrid's accomplishments, whatever they might be, or utterly indifferent to them.

Then one evening, not long after dinner, a strange sequence of sounds. Normally at a friend's place to practice at that time, Ingrid happened to be in that evening on account of a bad stomach. The first two sounds, two-part prologue, were moments apart: Father's footsteps in the kitchen and a short, muted but infinitely anguished cry from Ingrid's room. Then the adagio of the faucet taps turning, and some rapid thumping, the sound of running downstairs, giving release to the pulse of water and the gradually building squeaking of the pipes, an escalation suddenly halted with a flat sound of hollow expiration, as though a serpent coughed its last. The water in which Father was washing his hands disappeared.

Father did not play the piano that evening.

A plumber came to the house the next day and Father conferred with him; when he left, Father confined himself to his study. Ingrid had left the house very early that morning and as the day wore on, everyone talked of dinner, and every question and speculation about what was to be served was understood not to concern food. The silence was terrible. Father's fury was certain: though never before glimpsed or guessed at by any in the house, his temper surely blazed behind his general severity of manner. One of the smallest children could not be consoled, so apprehensive did she become that afternoon, and she had to be repeatedly told that the plumbing problem of the previous evening was an obscure accident and promised an extra sweet after dinner in order to restore her face's proper colour.

Ingrid arrived at the table right before Father himself did and she had, if it were possible, assumed an even more remote comportment. None of the glances from across and along the table, compassionate or curious, were so much as noticed. She stood, as everyone did, when Father entered, but with the expression of someone thinking through some distant, intractable, but dispassionately observed problem.

As soon as everyone was seated, Father poured himself his one constitutional half-glass of wine and cleared his throat. He cast an inscrutable look around the table, settling on no one, as though he were simply taking stock, and then launched forth the longest speech anyone could recall ever having heard him make. Indeed, for years afterward many in the house would have been able to recite it word for word.

In the village in which my own father was born, Father said, it was for many generations the custom that, on a particular spring day, the tall trees of the village were to be treated not just deferentially but as august personages. From sunrise to sundown on that day, they were addressed as My Lord or My Lady, or even Your Eminence or simply Sir or Madame, as one preferred. One doffed one's hat or even bowed low in passing them and their pardon was begged if one walked between them. There was no extreme to this deference, Father said with his hands firmly pressed together. No gesture, he said, could be too respectful to the trees, and no one deviated from this custom – until one day, someone did just that.

I am quitting my studies at the Institute, Ingrid said.

After a few moments in which none spoke, she excused herself from the table and could be heard putting on her coat. As she went out and the door closed behind her, an obscure relative seated far from Father squeaked his opinion that arboreal concerns were lost on the young, which statement Father cut very short with another, much more vigorous clearing of his throat, and a long reach for the bread basket. A few subsequent attempts at dinner conversation were likewise aborted.

The events of these two evenings were together known as the second of Ingrid's scenes, a term only employed when Father was out of earshot, and then always with a combination of bewilderment, giddy embarrassment, and awe. Yet it was the third scene that caused the most consternation.

Father played the piano each day following the evening of the dinner of his uncharacteristic speech and Ingrid's interruption, seemingly working at the same piece, though no one was entirely certain of that. At any rate, his assiduity was as evident as Ingrid's absence at dinners. She was seen to come and go from the house very occasionally, never impolite but aloof and quick to leave again. After a week or so of this uneasy routine, the piano-tuner was called in and, unusually, ushered to Father's study. The door was closed for nearly an hour, a little longer, perhaps, than any of the piano-tuner's previous visits, and when it reopened both men were flushed and frowning.

A number of convoluted, sometimes wild theories were ventured when Father next left the house. One suggested that the piano-tuner had corrupted Ingrid – perhaps ruined her in a way that some in the house understood with dread and horror and the rest could not quite understand but nonetheless contemplated with dread and horror – and Father was rightly outraged, demanding that the honourable thing be done, whatever it might be. Another view held that the piano-tuner had, however belatedly, acquiesced to Ingrid's demands and taken it away – allowing considerable room for further theorization about what "it" referred to, how it was taken away, and when – and Father, having discovered it gone, accused the thief. The darkest theory, especially popular with the excitable twins, conjectured that Father had murdered Ingrid and enlisted the piano-tuner's help in disposing of the body, which was perhaps hidden in the piano. No theory was too incredible.

This new daily piano regimen ended when Ingrid again took her place at the dinner table, and thereafter there seemed to be some unspoken agreement – though no one would have dared to call it that – about Ingrid not being in the house when Father elected to play the piano, or if there were no such agreement, in any event the two did not coincide. Dinner conversations in those days might lengthily deliberate on the price of timber or settle for an unsettling moment on this or that young one's performance at school, but neither music nor Ingrid's abandonment of her studies were even obliquely mentioned, a chilling fact that made everyone at the table, save Ingrid and, less apparently, Father, all the more willing to press on with the alternative subjects, so it might be said that dinner conversations thereafter became more genial, warm, and relaxed even as they became more constrictive, tepid, and forced. Autumn came and went in this way.

No one has forgotten the great snowstorm of that year, though its screeching winds and hourly mounting snowbanks were prelude, for everyone in the house, of what was most frozen in memory. After four days of unceasing snow, the house was marooned, barricaded, the windows pasted with white. None of the sober doors to the outside would so much as budge but the temperature raced drunkenly downward. Neither the postman nor the piano-tuner was to be seen. However, the dutifully humming furnace was never a concern and the larder contained plenty of supplies.

How long, everyone silently wondered, read that question in each other's faces, how long? How long could the Muse, if that's what it was, be kept stifled? Each evening Father emerged from his study a little more haggard and wan, arriving at the dinner table just a few moments later than the evening before, as though his sense of tempo was gone, and Ingrid, who with everyone else was all the more pointedly punctual at the dinner hour, could be seen to be watching him closely, but her own formidable reserve made it impossible to detect what she might be thinking as she watched. The cold outside governed absolutely, in a way that Father himself perhaps never had. Five nights locked in, no playing of the piano and no piano-tuner and no piano of yours; six nights; seven.

On this seventh night, the conversation ran out and was

replaced with efforts to contain sighs and yawns. Father stirred his dinner more than he partook of it, his dark, terribly weary-looking eyes, like those of a disproved god, occasionally examining the disheveled appearance or the conspicuous lack of character of someone at the long table. When at last his eyes came to Ingrid, she surprised everyone by speaking. Father, she said, without the slightest hint of a conciliatory or even gentle tone. Father, she said, tell us, would you, about the custom in your father's village, long ago, of paying homage to the tall trees.

Father glanced at his plate, as though to consult its advice, and gradually shook his head.

There was a day, a specific spring day, wasn't there, Ingrid continued, her volume increasing, a day in which everyone in the village raised their hats to the tall trees and bowed to them and called them Sir and Madame.

Father was not responding, his plate yet his silent counsel.

It was the custom, Ingrid said, very loudly now but still without any emotion whatsoever in her voice, it was a custom observed throughout the village, wasn't it, and no one failed to observe it, that's what you said, but why, Father, why was it the custom, why did everyone follow this rule on this one particular day?

Ingrid, someone coughed, Ingrid, please. Another voice told her that she was distressing Father, was she really so insensitive to that fact, and her mouth closed. Father looked down the table, perhaps to see who had spoken, but his gaze fixed on no certain place, and he stood up uneasily, and everyone rose with him and watched as he slowly left the room.

Only a few days later, when the wind and cold abated, or at least passed on to trouble another house, Ingrid departed without any notice. She left behind whatever clothes did not fit into her one large suitcase, as well as her violin and flute. A pair of distant cousins, whose almost constant fighting with one another did not particularly ingratiate them to anyone else, wasted no time in taking her room. In the course of one of their squabbles they broke both the violin and the flute. Their bruised and swollen eyes were fearfully closed and their scratched and bandaged arms trembled when they were brought to apologize to Father, but he absolved them with an absent wave of his large hand and said nothing.

This may have been a grievous mistake for, the following month, that same pair were found setting fire to the piano, which Father had not touched since the beginning of the terrible snow-storm. An accident, the cousins unwaveringly pleaded, though occasionally one would confide that the accident was primarily the fault of the other. The piano-tuner came to see the patient, though no one knew who called him and Father was not at home to meet him. Your piano is very old and does not deserve such treatment, he scolded those at home to hear him.

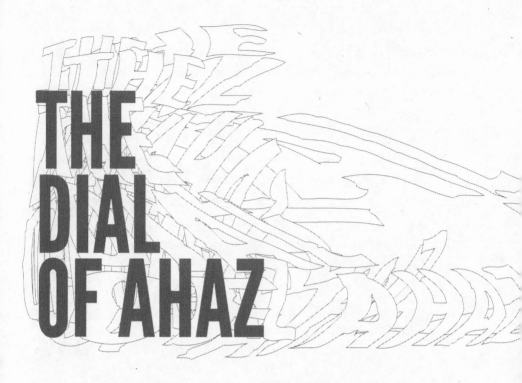

# THE DIAL OF AHAZ

And Hezekiah said unto Isaiah, What *shall* be the sign that the LORD will heal me, and that I shall go up into the house of the LORD the third day?

And Isaiah said, This sign shalt thou have of the LORD, that the LORD will do the thing that he hath spoken: shall the shadow go forward ten degrees, or go back ten degrees?

And Hezekiah answered, It is a light thing for the shadow to go down ten degrees: nay, but let the shadow return backward ten degrees.

And Isaiah the prophet cried unto the LORD: and he brought the shadow ten degrees backward, by which it had gone down in the dial of Ahaz.

And Hezekiah said unto Isaiah, What *shall* be the sign

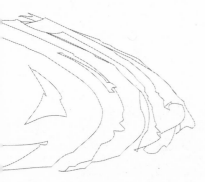

that the LORD will heal me, and that I shall go up into the house of the LORD the third day?

And Isaiah said, This sign shalt thou have of the LORD, that the LORD will do the thing that he hath spoken: shall the shadow go forward ten degrees, or go back ten degrees?

And Hezekiah answered, It is a light thing for the shadow to go down ten degrees: nay, but let the shadow return backward ten degrees.

And Isaiah the prophet cried unto the LORD: and the LORD did give answer: Why ask thou for what hath been given unto thee?

And Isaiah was in a mighty confusion, and bit his lip and his beard.

# DEDICATION

This next number I want to dedicate to Maddy Baumgarten. Some of you, I don't know how many know Maddy, but she has been a very important person in my life personally. Just to begin with, Maddy bought me my first guitar. This isn't the guitar in question. About four years ago there was a fire in the apartment where I was living and I really lost everything. Imagine losing everything, or if you have lost everything, then you don't have to imagine it, but just, it's awful and you feel lost. Maddy bought me a guitar, or well she helped me buy it, she was the driving force, and that was a whole new start for me. You have to understand that at that point, when I was living in the apartment, I was in a pretty bad scene, lots of negative stuff going on in my life, not that I want to get into all of that here, but you can take my word for it, not good. There was this guy I was kind of seeing and he was bad news, but I didn't see it at first, and anyway I don't want to get into all that. Back then I wasn't even writing songs. There was some drug involvement, and that got out of hand

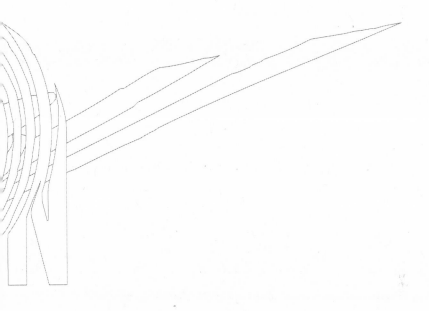

pretty quickly, maybe some of you know about that, saw me back
then, or maybe from your own life experience. Maybe you can't see it
but my retina was what they call compromised, don't you like that, a
nice way of saying damaged but without saying that, bad life deci-
sions, whole other story. Well, like I said, I lost everything in that
fire, was lucky to get out with my life, and not long after that Maddy
took me aside and said, you are a phoenix. I mean I had no ideas
what she was talking about, all I was thinking about was how can I
score, but I don't want to score, and I hate Donny but he could probably get something together, and memories of the fight, so I had no
idea at all what she was talking about, and then I found out that a
phoenix, maybe some of you know this, was this mystical bird that
was reborn in fire. And that's what Maddy was telling me: I had to
become a phoenix, I had to be reborn, I had to survive the fire and
become a new person, let the fire make me a new person. So I began
reading a load of stuff about the phoenix and fire rituals and what

different world cultures have believed about what fire is, about the power of flames. And this led me to this website for this kind of organization, the Friends of the Flame, and these people meet for these rites, and I started talking with them in chatrooms and found out about them. They were really accepting and most of them had some serious baggage that they said they were burning away in these rites, and I told Maddy about it, and she said, interesting. So she agreed to kind of escort me to the next meeting of the Friends of the Flame, which was down in Oregon, and Maddy drove, she has this sensible car she takes everywhere, I don't know how many of you know it or have seen it. Apparently she got it for almost exactly nothing and it never needs to be fixed. And so we drove down to Oregon and I met some people who were only virtual to me up to that point. Everybody in the Friends agrees to go by these new fire names they've chosen, and there was already a girl there named Phoenix so I eventually settled on Combustible, which was Scorch's suggestion, this pretty cute guy who turned out to be, well, I'll get to that in a way, because in a way this is all part of the next song I'm going to sing for you. Anyway, Maddy was there as an observer, she said, but she later told me that she was secretly tape recording a lot of what was going on. So there was this big dinner out under the night sky and some singing by a big fire, which was probably my first use of this, this is the guitar in question I played that night, and then there was this kind of meditation and prayer thing, and there was some drugs too but nothing I couldn't handle, but then everyone started taking off their clothes and I knew, like, something was not right. They were throwing their clothes in the fire and I kind of got into the spirit of it because it was fun, right, but Maddy and her tape recorder weren't there because she kind of hooked up with this guy Sparky in a tent somewhere. You can still see it, right, right here, this finger doesn't go straight any more. So it was a trauma. And you think about that, it won't go away, and all I could think of for a long time after that was this boyfriend I used to have, years ago, not the one in the apartment but still a total, total loser. He actually went camping with me and a few friends one summer and when I got really sick and nearly died choking on my own vomit, sorry for the graphic detail but it was all pretty awful, we were all doing vodka that night, he and a friend, a girlfriend of mine were getting it on and pretty loudly, too, all night long in the tent next to mine where I was practically dying. You know how some nights you look up at the stars, and believe me they have some amazing starry nights in Oregon, and you think, none of you cares, none of you gives a shit, but you're still beautiful. How can they be beautiful and not give a shit? I had to crawl out of the tent, kind of on my elbows because my hands were burned from this accident with the bonfire, no need to get into that, and I would crawl out just to, you know, throw up, and I'd roll over and look at the stars and talk to them like that in my head, partly to stop thinking about the shape I was in and partly to block out the sounds from the tent next to mine going all night long. Later on, months after that when I was pretty seriously involved with this online chatroom about lost destinies, this one contact of mine who was accredited, that's probably not the word I want but let's say accredited with some divination abilities, not major but serious enough, believe me. She told me that Combustible was a good name but not for me, not for my self but for my false self, the one that everyone's always trying to sell you or force on you or expects from you, and I wasn't sure what to make of that because I was just then seeing this guy who was into science, not a professional scientist but he was into gravity, this big cosmic force. Did you know that even though it's this big cosmic force, gravity is really, really weak? It holds all these planets and stars together, orchestrates them was the word this guy, Pender, he would say orchestrates, a musical word, and that's probably the sort of thing that drew me to him. Naturally I didn't know that he was married, married to this woman whose bags of money and piles of jewellery gave her the right to be rude to absolutely everyone, I mean maybe I should have, I mean, chalk that up as a life lesson, right? And I should never have agreed to the photos thing, but let's not get into, I mean it was total exploitation one way or another and there's nothing more to be said about that. But I looked at some of his science books, astronomy books and thought, well, here's another belief system that I don't understand so well, and so I got into a confused state and I was very much in that state when I met up with Maddy at this rally, that was Vancouver two years ago, in the fall. And Maddy could see I was pretty messed up, not just because of the cast on my leg from the bike accident, free safety tip to everyone, don't, absolutely do not bike when you're stoned on stuff you've never really tried before, and to be completely honest some of that messed-upness was probably residual emotional stuff from Oregon, because actually the girlfriend of mine that night was Maddy, and I eventually forgave Maddy for that but this loser, the one in the tent, Donny, not Sparky, but she was with him in a tent, just not the same tent, not the same occasion. I don't want you to get the impression that I only sleep in tents! Though now that I think about it. I mean, I don't have a lot of material attachments, a big fire wiping out your whole material life kind of takes care of that, a fire sermon like the Buddhist thing, very instructive and no questions afterwards. The big fire —which basically I guess I kind of unconsciously was the one who started – killed my cat, Shadow, and I was thinking of how all these symbols were circling around me, gravity and fire and the false self and the shadow and the stars, so beautiful but they don't give a shit. And I said to Maddy, what does it mean? And Maddy didn't understand at first, she just said it's only sex, what else have we got, and I told her I wasn't angry and she asked why not, and I said anger's not me, I won't let anger be me. By then I knew that she had been blackmailing Pender and I was pretty sure that she had slept with him a few times while we were together, and that explains how he was always losing our money in what he said were good investments, but that's not exactly relevant right now. I told her about the weakness of gravity and the possibility that my real self perished in the fire or maybe that my hands burning that time was a reminder that fire wasn't done with me yet and I told her about the orchestration. We were celebrating her getting this publishing deal for this book, this novel she's been writing for years and now it's finally going to come out and I can't wait to see it. She asked me if I still had that guitar she had given me, and I wondered at first what does that have to do with anything but said, the guitar you bought for me when you called me the phoenix, and she laughed and said yes, but before I could say anything more I was startled, I could have sworn that I saw Shadow's eyes in her eyes, she told me that the guitar was actually stolen, she had stolen it from this music store years ago. This guitar, this isn't the guitar in question. But I'd like to play this song, the song I've just told you about, I'd like to play it for you now.

# BUT FOR A MEASURING ROD

An optometrist goes to see another optometrist. I have judged over two hundred patients legally blind in the past month, he explains, and that startling figure either signifies some kind of a phenomenon or necessitates that I get my own vision checked. You're too hard on yourself, always have been, laughs his compeer. He draws the blinds, points to the chart, and says, You know what to do. The troubled optometrist, let us call him Alpha, tells the examining optometrist, let us call him Not-Alpha, that the chart is too familiar to him, all the standard-issue charts their offices use are too familiar to serve as a reliable test for him, who could recite them without knowing for sure whether he saw each letter clearly or not. You're right, Not-Alpha agrees, a touch grudgingly because he himself never remembers the charts, even though he's seen them and heard them read to him literally thousands of times.

So this second optometrist takes the first to a strip club on the outskirts of town, and asks him if he notices anything unusual

54

there. The drinks are kind of pricey, says Alpha. Not what I had in mind and irrelevant to the question at hand, Not-Alpha retorts and gestures to one of the performers onstage. Have you noticed her? His companion cranes his neck and studies a swaying woman in her early twenties, if he is any judge of age, though in truth he is not. Says optometrist Not-Alpha in his ear, Read to me what's written across her belly, and he sees that yes indeed there is as it were cunei-form script gently striping her there. Her bobs and undulations naturally shape the rhythm of his reading aloud the following:

*Created at twilight, before the Sabbath, it was given to Adam in the Garden of Eden. Adam gave it to Chanoch, who gave it to Metushelach; he in turn passed it on to Noach. Noach bequeathed it to his son Shem, who transmitted it to Avraham. From Avraham to Yitzchak, and then to Ya'aqov, who took it with him to Egypt. Ya'aqov gave it to Yosef; upon Yosef's death all his possessions were removed to Pharaoh's place. Yitro*

*one of Pharaoh's advisors desired it, whereupon he took it and stuck it in*
*the ground in his garden in Midian. From then on no one could pull out*
*the staff until Moshe came. He read the Hebrew letters on the staff, and*
*pulled it out readily.*

Not-Alpha claps him on the shoulder: Your eyes seem fine to me.
But that's an extraordinary tattoo, says Alpha, still staring, and
no sooner has he uttered these words than a third man promptly
sits down with them and introduces himself as a dermatologist. I
couldn't help noticing your attention to Mitzi, he says, hooking a
thumb at the stage, which the remarkable woman now exits. If I'm
not mistaken, you're admiring the writing on her skin, and that is
to say that you recognize those markings for what they are, writing,
and there seem to be few enough among the patrons who manage
to do so. It's an extraordinary tattoo, repeats the first optometrist,
who introduces himself and his associate. Not to diminish your feat
of reading quite accurately those tiny letters in lighting and from
a distance and within an environment not at all conducive to such
concentration, chuckles the dermatologist, your senses deceive you
somewhat. The dermatologist's chuckle is irritating, and though
neither of the optometrists says anything about it he can see plainly
enough it has irritated them, and knows from a lifetime of ill-ad-
vised chuckles that the sound he thus emits is irritating for almost
everyone, save his wife, who may very well be lying about it.

The dermatologist diplomatically leads the optometrists from
the noisy strip club down the night street smeared with garish lights
to a coffee shop where they can talk. Alpha and Not-Alpha exchange
a look that says, We're both curious, though we probably shouldn't
be, about this Mitzi, but the air of secrecy to this man's conversation
is hard to fathom and besides, his chuckle is irritating, but notwith-
standing this expressive shared look they join him at a booth and
order coffees from a waitress who coughs rather than speaks. That
tattoo, says Alpha the optometrist the moment the waitress has
left them with their steaming cups, what is all that about? I mean I

read it, but to be blunt with you, it's been a long time since my bar mitzvah, you see what I'm saying. Not-Alpha nods vigorously and wants to know what kind of girl so religious as to imprint her body with it takes up that kind of work. And isn't that, well, kind of *tameh*, I guess is the expression? The dermatologist blows on his coffee to cut off the urge to chuckle again. It's amazing how many of you have been trickling into that place in the past three or four weeks to get an eyeful of her, he says. What do you mean, how many of us? Us what? Not-Alpha asks. Optometrists, replies the dermatologist, and I must correct you from the start: it's not a tattoo. It is an undiagnosed skin condition.

In the few moments of silence that follow this pronouncement all three men stare into their respective coffees. In his coffee, optometrist Alpha sees the rippling letters and words he has read only a short while ago, dancing on that perfect dancing body, and feels himself absorbed by this image, while Not-Alpha finds in his coffee an unconsoling blackness that somehow testifies to his inability to recollect those standard eye charts or even the text of Mitzi, to which he had brought this other man, who sees further and retains better, even as he is falling into this blinding blackness. The dermatologist is unsurprised to see his wife's face in his coffee looking up at him. She is always telling him he should drink less coffee. When next he speaks, it is as though he is addressing someone not at the table.

Mitzi Messer was, he reveals, by all accounts a good girl from a home never broken nor even threatened with breakage, went to a school with no more than the usual and perhaps prerequisite number of bullies, dunces, and mortally bored teachers, where she did respectably well and had no serious upsets to her equilibrium until one day in the swimming pool changeroom she discovered this strange outbreak across her midsection. Her parents brought the doctor, the doctor brought more confusion, accusing them of mocking him and, he added, as he really got going, all of medical science. The family's respect for this professional all too quickly became terrified efforts at deference, but he would have none of it and hastened his querulous march towards retirement without so much as a glance behind, never mind a referral. Mitzi's mother had a cousin in medical school who agreed to stop in one weekend, and that turned out to be a weekend none of them would forget. The cousin, up till then a pretty stable sort with a good wife of three years and a nice career ahead of him, called his wife the first night and told her it was over, he was in love with another woman, his cousin's daughter all right but it wasn't like that, and she should never expect to hear from him again, may the heavens bless her, and all of this in the most pseudo-Talmudic jargon about purity and transformation and whatever else. And after may the heavens bless you he hung up. He had talked, his wife later said, as though he had turned into a blend of throbbing adolescent and stentorian rabbi. The very next night he packed in a hurry, fled the house without goodbyes to his cousin, and drove home to sob for forgiveness. Mitzi by all accounts was almost traumatically upset, but totally withdrawn, wouldn't discuss what had happened with anyone, and within the week she had moved out herself without a word to anybody.

She went to New Jersey first, says the dermatologist, his face all unmistakable wonderment as to why anyone would do that. She told me that, one of the few details of her life I have directly from her. It was nearly a year ago that I first met her, but it wasn't in that place she's working in now. Not my usual sort of hangout, or at least I would have said so back then, but to be frank I find myself there two or three nights a week now, sometimes more. What I tell everyone, myself included, is that I'm spending my nights doing research, which is true from a certain point of view, especially if research is searching for something of which you vaguely suspect you once had an understanding.

Not-Alpha waves a hand: It's not that I don't believe you. What is it exactly that you deny not believing? the dermatologist asks the waving hand. His trained eye can see that the optometrist once suffered the effects of poison ivy. Is it New Jersey you don't believe? I don't see why she would lie about it. There could be a connection, interjects the first optometrist, Alpha, between all those people losing their sight and this skin condition. I mean, there could be, right? You said that that particular club fills up with optometrists. And dermatologists, answered the dermatologist sadly, and psychologists and speech therapists. I once met a chiropractor in one of the dives she used to work in and I no longer view that as a coincidence. Not-Alpha's hand repeats its dance more vigorously: It's not that I don't believe you. But he says nothing more. He is thinking about how it was his bright idea to bring his friend to this club and look at this dancer, let's be honest, this stripper, and whatever had possessed him to do a thing like that?

The brief silence is interrupted by the waitress, who is still brandishing a pot of coffee. Languidly chewing gum, she says scornfully, You guys seem so depressed, you know, it's depressing just looking at you guys. The dermatologist shrugs and says something about how they are more actually confused than depressed, and the waitress shifts the pot to her left hand and puts the right in a fist against her hip. Naw, you're depressed, it's written all over you, you know. I can read people. We've just been talking about reading people, chirps Not-Alpha, who is almost always stirred to a defensive cheeriness of manner when he is accused of being depressed. The waitress makes a short toot of a laugh and her gum-chewing speed increases just slightly. Is that a fact? Let me tell you, all right, we used to get this customer in here all the time, guy who was really depressed all the time, you know, and the funny thing was he used to tell me he was confused. He was in here all the time, always down in the dumps, and him and me used to talk about it, and at first he said there was something like a miracle he'd witnessed, you know, that was what he said. She chews a few times for emphasis and the three men try not to be obvious about their exchange of looks and thereby each is left unsure exactly what the looks from the other two are supposed to mean. She anticipates a question.

What miracle? asks the first optometrist. This appears to be the wrong question for the waitress frowns and reverses the arrangement of hands and coffee pot but does not slow the chewing. Like I'm going to ask about that, she says flatly. But it doesn't matter because after a while, after he's been in here a few times, in fact at about this time of night, and him and me would get talking, and it turned out, you know, that he's depressed behind being confused, if you see what I mean, and then we get right down to it and he tells me, not all at once of course, that his prostate is all filled up with cancer and his kid hasn't called him in almost ten years and he's worried his new landlord is going to evict him, and I tell him, you know, of course you're confused and depressed, of course you're seeing miracles, you want to see miracles, you don't want to see what's right in front of you, you know, like the writing's on the wall. She nods and drifts away to other tables where coffees await freshening.

So there they are, these three wise men, thinking about what one doesn't see and about scratches that can't be itched, and even though those are, when you come to think of it, optometrical and dermatological concerns, none of them is comforted by the fact. Each one is wondering: will I be here tomorrow night, after taking in the show? What about the night after that? Is this coffee going to keep me up all night tonight, never mind the thoughts in my head, what I have seen and heard this night?

Wise men! Life is tough. Take the guy the waitress mentioned, Danny Sachs, all-around *mensch* with just fifty-one years on his back, this same night in terrible, terminal pain in a sub-par hospital on the other side of town, shrieking down the halls: *So pull it out, already!*

# ATTENTION TO DETAIL

At just the moment that Kevin and Wes were faced with the awkward situation of having their statements of wager about whether Lindsay from Finance's breasts were real or not interrupted by the arrival at their table of Kimberly, lunch-laden tray in hand, asking with a tone not unqualified by irony whether she might join them, a few feet above them a schism opened as though the very fabric of the atmosphere had been ripped open and the many spurred tentacles of unknown Forces of Darkness quickly, clumsily, hungrily reached down and seized hold of Kevin, who barely managed the breath for a scream as he was yanked into the extraordinary aperture above, which immediately closed thereafter with awful soundlessness.

For very nearly a week after this incident talk in the cafeteria was of almost nothing else.

"Maybe it's a metaphor."

"Kevin was all right, you know?"

"I think you mean *allegory*."

"I think I chipped my tooth."

All of this information came to me from my lover of that time, a zaftig custodian who regularly sponged up what crumbs and stains the suits left behind. We had met at a stag and doe and at length united in the view that there are aspects of Billy Joel's oeuvre not yet appreciated, but two months into things she attempted to prevent my attentions from wandering with tales from the workplace.

"Must have been pretty quick after that that a new opening in Design was posted because I swear just a week later there's this new galoot in the cafeteria every lunchtime, tall like you've never seen, always by his lonesome, never eating with anybody else, and so what was I to do but wonder and then Edie who usually works the register there told me he doesn't pay for his food but he's got this special card from the company that puts everything on account, and the strangest thing is that he puts ketchup on everything, and I mean everything, from salad to soup and cookies and pie, loads and loads of ketchup so now they have to refill the dispenser every week."

This is a truncated transcript of what she actually said. At the time she was speaking, I was not listening with full attention but rather thinking

*pom pom pom purr pom*
*pom pom*
*zeek zeek errompom pom pom*
*zeek zeek*
how lovely are the *brum de drum*
*dee drum drum*

and before I knew it, she had fled the apartment with all of the credit cards, some of them still useable. Impossible to say what was more upsetting: the potential financial fallout, the (surely transitional) loneliness, or the dissatisfaction of not knowing the rest of the story.

Nothing easier than to console the widow (if widow she was), but calling every Kevin in the telephone book ate up a week with nothing to show for it except regular return calls from an especially garrulous Kevin who "just could not get over" how "we really clicked" in that one brief telecommunication. Aha – contact the ketchup producers! Summary of conversation: hello, hello, do you supply ketchup locally, yes, and could you confirm reports of an exponential demand, may I ask who, am with the Condiments Quality Agency (CQA), not familiar with it, tirelessly verifying integrity of product and safety and satisfaction of consumers our mandate, ah, surprising how many adulterations of ketchup occur, ah, currently studying reasons for apparent addiction-near consumption levels particularly among executives, ah, possible correlation to productivity, please hold. Why not get a job as a courier and wait for the inevitable letter to be delivered to the Design offices, get right in there and see with one's own eyes? Three weeks and two painful bicycle accidents later comes the brilliant additional idea to pseudonymously post that letter myself rather than wait for one that might never come, but this cherry popsicle of a plan melts off the stick when fast upon follows the recognition that I knew not one full name of a single employee nor even the name of the company. My (former) custodian had surely uttered the last many times in my hearing but, wouldn't you know, at every such moment

*pom pom*

*pom pom purr brum de dum*

and so on. For more or less similar reasons the courier company eventually fired me.

Loneliness.

Weeks of it, to the tune of two. But the experience (silent nights of cold cereal) allowed for its very study, leading to a very good definition, or what seemed like a good definition at the time. Loneliness is the awareness of the story being elsewhere, of your being outside of, remote from, the ongoing story, of knowing that it is going on without you. Some equilibrium had perhaps been struck when one man had been snatched from one story and thrust into another, or perhaps it was an exchange, Kevin for the Ketchup Man, trading stories – but what was any of that to me, locked out of all of these stories, counting ceiling tiles?

"There's another way to look at it," said the wide-eyed woman in the cereal aisle of the supermarket. "Loneliness is as much a delusion as community, if one considers the simultaneous co-existence of stories, as you so *faux*-naively put it, made so dramatically evident by this mid-lunch abduction of an office factotum into some unknown other plane, one must concede the not simply open but wide-yawning possibility that yet other dimensions of yet other ongoing stories may well exist beyond our detection, and thus we are each of us wholly outside of countless stories, to continue using your term, and because we, like your Kevin – "

"He's not *my* Kevin. I've never met him and have no connection to him. I'm not even sure that's his name."

She gave me a look that managed to be pitying, withering,

and amused all at once, and promptly pushed her shopping cart round the corner and was gone. Gone, that is, in the sense that I probably could have found her elsewhere in the store or even laid in wait by the row of check-out registers had the cinnamon buns not been on sale.

Cinnamon buns! *bun bun dum dee dum.*

# CLOSER STILL

The gentleman came in and very calmly and deliberately sized up the place. He gave Brzni a nod when his eyes fell to him, and the same to Rejk, who was in his usual place. Declining to remove his jacket, the gentleman sat down on the bench and waited his turn while Brzni finished Voyra's boy. He sat with his hands folded in his lap, the very picture of tranquil waiting, and Rejk carried on telling Brzni why restaurants fail, and Brzni chimed in with his own insights: cleanliness is paramount; there is no question that building up a steady clientele and offering a rich and unique menu are extremely important, but cleanliness is paramount. Rejk emphasized what he called atmosphere, which led the barber to observe that atmosphere is nothing without cleanliness, that cleanliness is the basis for atmosphere. But atmosphere is more than cleanliness, countered Rejk, who picked up and then put down again the rolled newspaper he forgot that he had brought with him.

    The newspaper said it would be a sunny day, very season-

able, not a cloud to be seen though a little rain might fall by the end of the week; and the wording of a proposed new bylaw about dog leashes was causing some trouble for legislators and dog-walkers alike, since it effectively said that all dogs not on a leash were to be leashed by their owners, but did not say what was to be done with those dogs that had no owners, regardless of whether or not they were on a leash; and a helicopter that had crashed nearly a week ago was found to have malfunctioned, though sabotage and by implication attempted murder had not been entirely ruled out; and its special supplement on radishes included a lively pictorial history of the subject, notes on the various kinds of radishes and how they are grown, an ode to radishes written by a clever student, and a few recipes for cider, soup, and assorted pastries.

The door's chime jingled again while Brzni was saying that he had a lot of sympathy for anyone trying to get a start in the restaurant business. In came another gentleman, who quickly scanned the shop and sat down on the bench next to the first. This second gentleman's indistinguishability from the first in every detail, from polished shoes to unremoved jacket and from pointed chin to folded hands, was initially observed only by Voyra's young son, who gave a little toot of ambiguous amusement and was gently reminded by the barber to sit still. Rejk remarked that the word restaurateur was an answer in the crossword the other day, unnecessarily adding as he always did on these occasions that regularly doing the crossword helped stave off the disintegration of one's intellectual faculties.

A framed picture on the wall smiled indiscriminately at everyone. The face, which belonged to Brzni's daughter, or had belonged to her some four or five years ago when the photograph was taken, was reddened by the sun that was probably setting behind the invisible photographer, which effect made it seem a little younger than it was, but anyone would agree with the description girlish, and in fact when the barber referred to her it was always as a girl, a wonderful girl, my wonderful girl. The photograph was taken in Australia, a few months after she moved there, but when asked Brzni has been unable to say exactly where in Australia, though of course he acknowledges that it is a very big country, but the thing is the girl moves around all the time and he can never remember all of the place names anyway. The face in the photograph looked warm and happy. Her neck and shoulders, also visible, might have been tanned but the redness of the light makes it hard to be certain.

When Rejk's father was slowly dying, he remembered aloud, his intellectual faculties had disintegrated; he did not recognize his sons, he did not know what day or month it was, he did not know he was no longer in his home. Rejk was about to recount his last visit to his hospitalized father when he noticed that the two customers sitting on the bench, patiently waiting for Brzni to finish that pushy woman's son, looked absolutely identical. At first he grunted, not altogether aware whether to be impressed by this phenomenon or irritated at losing what he was about to say, and Brzni took the opportunity to acknowledge that aging had little to recommend it.

70

He chuckled and the door to the barbershop jingle-jingled to let in a third gentleman with pointed chin and polished shoes, who nodded to Rejk and took a long look around the place before assuming the last remaining place on the bench.

Oh!

The boy's hair was taking too long. Both Brzni and his young customer were thinking this with some degree of irritation. The talk of aging prompted Brzni to wonder and worry, though his stony face showed none of it. Slow was all right so long as the job was well done, he thought, and thought about saying it aloud, so as to assure the boy, who was beginning to wriggle again, trying to see something in the mirror besides himself. Glancing at the clock, Brzni tried to remember when Voyra said she would be back to collect the boy: she was nothing if not punctual and precise. The boy likewise checked the clock. He was thinking of many things: that he would like to be a drummer; that the combs jarred in cerulean Barbicide looked like specimens of some alien life form; that the man talking to the barber probably did not know about the stains on his shirt, probably of soup or gravy; that the word for three identical people was triplets, and that he had never seen triplets before; that time was disappointing because it only went in the one direction; that the smell of the barbershop was not disagreeable; that black horses were more impressive than white horses; that as soon as he could he would leave school and become a pilot, if he could overcome his secret, paralyzing fear of heights.

There were several reasons why Rejk thought of the mother of the boy of some eight or nine years of age who was then having his hair cut as a pushy woman. Jing-jing-jingle said the chime on the door. The third barber chair in the shop had never been used, which is to say that in Brzni's recollection neither he nor his father before him had ever cut the hair of someone sitting in that particular chair, though perhaps that chair had been sat in on some occasion or other. The boy's hair was taking too long, Brzni nearly said it aloud, and looking back to the bench of customers he noticed that there were three gentlemen sitting there with a fourth politely standing next to them, all of them exactly alike. Almost finished, he said slowly, ostensibly to the boy or maybe to the waiting gentlemen. Rejk asked Brzni whether he had heard about the helicopter crash, how the pilot had not only survived but was entirely unhurt.

Do scissors snip? It sounds not quite right: snip snip, snip snip.

The mirror said, as it always had, different things to different people. To Voyra's son it hinted at the four gentlemen just out of sight while it more openly and blandly displayed all of the things behind him. To Rejk it made subtle suggestions about the ever-moreness of the world, as though to exhaust him, and he tried to pay it no attention, having had in any event little truck with mirrors for the past ten years or so. It reminded Brzni of the fragility of children, and then, as an afterthought, pointed out the four gentlemen, the door opening, the fifth gentleman. Brzni gestured, perhaps wordlessly because he could not at that moment think how to put the invitation into words, to the third barber chair, and then he thought of a way to respond to what his old friend had been telling him.

Brzni recounted, after clearing his throat, how his own father had passed away. No one could ever remember him ever being sick a day of his long life, but one winter's evening in his seventy-third year, after having put in his usual full day in the barbershop with his son and eaten his modest dinner, he went out for his customary walk. The narrative proper took a short hiatus as Rejk and the barber admired the benefits of walking, admitted that they themselves did not walk as much as they ought. Brzni's father's walk was routine, but his route was not: it varied from evening to evening, which was itself probably no small part of the habit's charm for the old man, and he liked to survey the neighbourhood and learn its byways and vertices. Depending on the variation, and perhaps what matters he was mulling over in his mind as he went, he could be out from an hour to three hours, a point about which his wife had for nearly forty years of marriage complained to everyone, unable to disguise her satisfaction in having no more serious grounds for complaint, until she had a heart complaint, and then the widower's walks comforted only his son. On this particular evening, jingle-jing-jingle, he had gone to the end of his own street, turned left, and followed that and each of the following four subsequent streets until it ended and there turned left, unless only a right turn were possible. He waved to old Ughrliya, who always admired his constitution, and a pair of children saw him just before he turned onto his final street, the street where he encountered the last sight anyone in his position could have reasonably expected to see.

She is in a hurry but it is all a misunderstanding. She can be calm and collected but there is a limit. All these excuses, she had said and he had said, these are conditions, not excuses, and they are obviously not mine. Her ankle hurts less vaguely than it had an hour ago. She remembered her uncle's speech, one of his rolling dinner table monologues, this one about the members of the legal profession, how they are impossible to get rid of, and therefore should rightly be identified as weeds. Always something else, and now it is raining and she is wearing this coat. Health inspection, she had said, when had this phrase been gloriously birthed into the language, health will not suffer to be inspected, it is what it is. It is not just that she does not want her son to see her upset but that she does not want the old barber and his cronies jabbering the days away to see her upset. Always something else, this clause on that form and then this other clause on that other form, there has to be a limit. Women on bicycles are undignified. It is raining. Her mother would have bowed down at the mere sight of the first obstacle, would have signed any paper put in front of her, but she would not. She would see it through. She smells the air and the rain and tries to slow down, to remember that it is, definitively, a misunderstanding, as definitively as it is raining, and it is definitively raining, she is walking to the barbershop in the very definition of rain. It does not drop, it falls.

Jingle-jingle.

Radishes can go a long way.

The aliens in the jar were probably sad, but at least they had each other.

Snip snip snip snipsnip snipsnip.

My son, my son.

To have escaped, to escape the crash, entirely unhurt.

Jingle-jingle.

Have each other.

Jingle-jing-snipsnip snip jingle.

Almost done, almost there.

Atmosphere.

# OBSERVING THE ARISTOTELIAN UNITIES

The five of us had been trapped in the elevator for nearly an hour when the excessively perspiring, bulky man who had hitherto been silent announced in

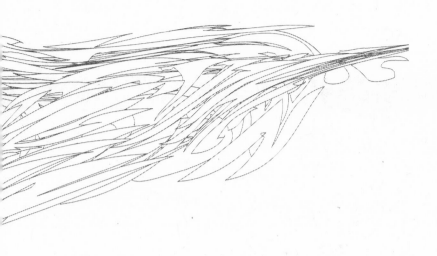

a most unhappy voice, "There's something I think you all should know."

# DO NOT REMOVE THIS TAG

When they come home the left shoe does not fit but the right does. The left shoe has shrunk, perhaps from embarrassment. Never mind, call the store. The number is no longer in service, a recording sympathizes and advises checking the number and trying the call again, ultimately to no purpose. Meanwhile the right shoe is perfect, they both look wonderful, it's a shame. The right shoe begins to sob, it's not its fault, but they are a team, it's a shame. Never mind, put them out of their misery. Down to the poorly lit basement, down to the even more poorly lit sub-basement. There the mangy goat waits. It does not know the meaning of second guesses. It has always uncomplainingly consumed the disappointments brought to it. No one remembers – and no one tries to remember – when the goat was first discovered there, tethered beneath the single dim bulb, or even a time when the goat has not been there, devouring the castoffs. What do those people down in the shabby trailers do? Surely they cannot have a sub-basement, and so they must live with their disappoint-

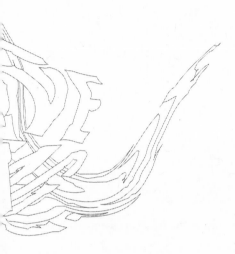

ments, which mutely wail all through the nights. Do you know, life is not very fair.

Then comes the day when a man from a government office calls to inspect the goat. Not just gumption, a real invasion of privacy. Of course he is told to mind his own so-called business and of course he says that's just what he's doing. He has cards and documents and an attache case and a head that does not move. Well, what would you do, bureaucrats are like a force of nature sometimes. Down to the poorly lit basement, all the while letting him know that this is unheard of, unnecessary, and down to the even more poorly lit sub-basement, him all the while silent to all this indignation, and there – not a goat, no goat at all, none in evidence, the dim bulb swaying above and the tether loose upon the clay below.

It is impossible to say from which direction the response first comes: where is; where have you hidden; who could have; know for a fact you have in your possession; always been right here; not to toy with the inspection office. A fluttering open of a notebook and the offence is documented. I shall return, he toots, I shall return within the week and if you cannot then produce to satisfaction the organism in question more serious action will be taken! They watch as he mounts the stairs and delivers a jolt of terror by turning his head to the side, once, sharply, looking back down at them for that half-second, as if to prove that he could and might turn his head further.

No time at all before suspicion collapses onto those people down in the shabby trailers, but nobody wants to knock on their dirty doors let alone admit the worst to them. Besides, let's think rationally a moment, there's no way they could have gotten past all the locks on the door let alone clambered up all the stairs obstinate stair-detesting animal in tow without being detected. It is hard to follow that moment, so we are still in it now, that long, long moment of thinking rationally, because as rational as we are we don't know how to get to that next moment until we get out of the rational, until we say, rationality sure is a killjoy, and then think or preferably do something irrational. This is how time progresses.

Left up to the smallest of the cousins. He smashes all of the dinnerware, probably has had it in mind for a long while, see it in how methodically yet swiftly he goes about it, and that gets time moving on again nicely. And before the shards and the reaction can settle, when melancholy is bound to move in at this destruction's reminder of the incomparable efficiency of the mangy goat, who would not have left a single shard to settle, before this can happen this same cunning one expertly sets fire to the drapes. They must be able to hear the cries of astonishment in Patagonia. How long has it been since possessions were seen burning? The question barely takes shape when sparks widen the spectacle and someone goes shouting for the kerosene.

And for a while – before the air runs out – it's like old times, redundancies wiped out, disappointments swallowed up, like things were. Only the smoke ruins it, with the goat there was never any smoke, call the fire department. The number is no longer in service, a recording sympathizes and advises checking the number and trying the call again, ultimately to no purpose.

# ME OR YOUR OWN EYES

## 1

The combination now had to be changed every week. When this latest news prompted Scrow to comment, his sullen partner, a man who once admitted to preferring sleep to most things life offered, gave his most noncommittal grunt. Their working relationship, in Scrow's opinion, was comparable to a vast balloon slowly, very slowly deflating.

"Surely there's a reason," he pressed, but saw that already Lemieux had turned his sheets of thought back and was climbing again into his comfy mental bed. They had been on the nightshift together at the gallery for nearly four months now; Scrow had had two and a half years of regular time under his belt before it dawned on him, abruptly and irrefutably, that he did not care much for people and especially despised children. One day after three exhausting school tours he requested a transfer. "Give me nights," he pleaded, "Before I crush one of those punks." Words to that effect.

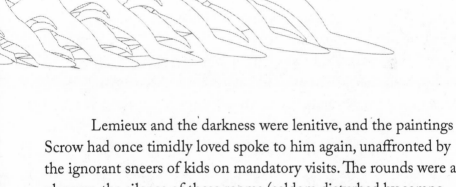

Lemieux and the darkness were lenitive, and the paintings Scrow had once timidly loved spoke to him again, unaffronted by the ignorant sneers of kids on mandatory visits. The rounds were a pleasure, the silence of these rooms (seldom disturbed by somnolent Lemieux) with their lights dimmed a gift. He found himself smoking much less, laughing at expressions and notions he genuinely thought funny, feeling healthier and lighter. Best of all, the rash that had covered most of his chest the months before the schedule change began to relent and fade. (For weeks the word *balm* regularly appeared in his thoughts, sometimes accompanied by a snatch of song: *Sometimes I feel so weary, and think my work's in vain ...* well, when Robeson did it it didn't sound silly.) Working nights meant not having to paw at himself inconspicuously and feel the burn without satisfaction. It was a miracle cure.

Or better. He remembered, with an excitement he locked his fingers to contain, the first time – how the air conditioning compelled his nipples to rise, sentinels thrilled that the territory between them was suddenly no longer retained by the enemy russet stain, as he unbuttoned his shirt and unclipped the tag with a photo of someone he recognized only in the daylight. How calm he had been, how he had actually folded each item and coiled the leather belt around the walkie-talkie, how it looked like a diminutive snake guarding what it mistook for its eggs. He unhooked and laid down his watch last, a digital made by his brother's company, and blinked at it with pity. Naked but for his glasses, Scrow almost pranced, nearly skated through the silent room.

At first he restricted this act – he had no name for it, just a loose collection of sensations and effects it would be somehow wrong to enumerate or analyze too fully – to a weekly routine, Thursday nights usually, and only after deluging Lemieux with greyest conversation in the early hours of the shift, to make sure he was good and bored. Scrow also tried different wings and rooms, until eventually he gave himself an hour and a half each night, by preference in the portrait galleries. There, amid the various stares of various court-goers of various centuries, he was most alive.

Nothing good can last, his wife had remarked three years before, and left him the following week. He was compelled to re-examine this anomalous pearl of wifely wisdom when the memoranda began to fall, new and newer notes and regulations. Leaden Lemieux offered no insights and their supervisor gave Scrow a discomfiting look when the guard asked (he had hoped casually) if there had been some specific problem prompting this greater vigilance.

"Let us worry about that," came the gravelly reply. "Just follow the procedures and keep your eyes open."

These procedures multiplied. Scrow reduced the number and frequency of his intimate visits with the portraits, while watching rather fiercely for anything irregular – be it an inexplicable pattern of dust or else a team of black-clad burglars suspended from grappling wires – in the hope of delivering it to his superiors who, with a placated smile, would then lower the alert level. Lemieux, on the other hand, seemed indifferent to the changes imposed upon his routine. Somehow, somewhere, he was still presumably sleeping on the job, and while he did so nothing awry, let alone sinister, interrupted Scrow's own bored patrols, and his few and timid disrobings were all too unsatisfying.

At last a compulsory set of staff meetings was scheduled. A stiff-jointed man introduced as Mister Duster, "security consultant," addressed the seated, cowed employees of the gallery. With what must have been emphatic pauses between clipped sentences, he politely took note of the past history of security measures taken by the gallery and, without unduly meditating upon the fact that no break-ins or thefts had ever been discovered, went on to suggest that these measures were inadequate by modern standards.

"If I may," Duster deliberated, "I would venture to ask of you, for example, what sort of protocols are set in place for the eventuality of a bomb threat?"

(*Balm* threat, Scrow thought involuntarily.)

When it became apparent that the silence which followed was not, this once, one of the consultant's rhetorical devices, a few heads shook before a young guard, his neck still marked with the acne of the previous season when he was hired, put up his hand and (leaving the hand lost in the air as he spoke) suggested calling the police. To this Duster sadly pressed his palms together in prayer fashion and gave a meaningful look to the board of directors and curators seated behind him on the dais. They collectively turned pale.

When more than two hours had passed and Duster had outlined his vision, his "plan of attack" as he called it, Scrow beat it to the washroom. Spot inspections, extended reports, passwords, and – the word had splat directly in Scrow's eye like the first hailstone of a terrible winter – cameras. His hands were shaking with the knowledge of what they would find as they loosed a couple of shirt buttons and exposed the rash, returned with a vengeance.

Cameras, a complete full video system wired throughout the

gallery, always awake, always alert, seeing and recording all. Scrow could not sleep because the cameras had already affixed themselves to the corners of his dreams. One by one his blankets, sheets, and pillows rubbed his skin the wrong way, turned it to sandpaper. Inflamed and locking his fingers together to prevent himself from madly scratching, he again poured tea and stared at the crumbs on the kitchen table. The microwave's clock would tell him, if he looked, that he had only a few hours before he had to go back to work and see for himself the technicians chewing gum and dismantling the former site of joy.

Wire, wire everywhere. They were there nights, too, in accord with the wish of the worried board of directors that the work be done quickly and the time that the gallery was closed to the public be kept to a minimum. They barked names back and forth, arms swinging. When they were not moving they were bantering loudly about nothing in particular – how life is unpredictable when it's not simply hard, paradoxically followed with notice of how good it is to be alive – as though to fill the space with action and noise, proof to themselves of their being there, of their existence. Scrow, always giving them a wide berth and seldom noticed, felt like a ghost watching the living insolently moving in and renovating his old haunt. As clanging tools struck the floor he would wince, at the same instant fretting and scratching his breast. One night as he took the last unthinking paces of his routine, blocking out the appalling manner in which a couple of the techies had within his earshot belittled the appearance of a full-necked woman who had probably been a courtesan paid to sit as someone nobler, a searing chord of pain was played across his stomach. He picked himself up from the floor at the same moment that weary hurrahs could be heard echoing between wings of the gallery. The surveillance system was operational.

2

Once, at a party she did not remember having been invited to, Emily overheard someone drunker than herself toss out the comment, "The problem with Napoleon Bonaparte was that he was under the grave delusion that he was Napoleon Bonaparte." Which one of the untenured yahoos she glanced at a moment later, each of whom was scarfing down popcorn so fast as to hamper proper breathing, had uttered this probably well-practiced quip did not, then or now, strike her as important. Yet some days after this party she found herself involuntarily drawn to the sentiment.

It had an immediate two-part explosive effect in her consciousness. The first and rather obvious reaction was a reverberating doubt, helped along by youth and a lively interest in recreational stimulants, that Emily Venture was actually Emily Venture. Perhaps she, like Bonaparte, was actually somebody else, conned into thinking otherwise, now acting out a role that History or some other less grand agency had assigned her. Mornings she would glare at the contents of her closet, second-guessing the choices she might be about to make. Was this particular blue truly her favourite colour, or did she simply not know better? Did tangerines appeal to her, or did she just imagine they did; would she prefer apples? Was there something phony about her laugh, and did she, the real she, even think that last joke funny?

Existentialist hijinks.

More bizarre and longer-lived was the subsequent anxiety; it was also less adolescent and self-regarding. What if, Emily hummed, all of those repeated images of the lunatic with hand snugly hidden at the chest and bicorn atop wide, white eyes were a revelation rather than a stereotype? The society, the psychological apparatus which denied that this or this man was Napoleon – or anyone other than who *it* said he was – suddenly seemed monstrous, oppressive, where once it had all seemed to her, if anything, innocuous, banal.

Surely Emily, if she were not Emily, could very well be Napoleon. True, she was not French and didn't even speak it (although, the devil's advocate would like to know, had she ever tried, really?). Nor was she, as men and women were given to remarking, at all short (but the phrase "commanding presence" might apply ...). And as for a burning desire to conquer Russia – well, no, but maybe only because she'd never given it much thought before. Specifics didn't matter, Napoleon didn't matter: *Napoleonness* was the thing.

For many important years, years her mother had warned her would shape her Character, Emily had this metaphysical monkey on her back. These were the years when she spent half her time studying history at an indifferent university and the other half dating an unusual series of men. She finished with each man when she determined that he was indeed who and what he thought and said he was, or at least when she became exhausted or bored by the effort. On only a couple of occasions did she try women, and found her customary methods confounded: neither of them had been exactly who and what they thought and it almost immediately became apparent that such was grounds for alarm. The second experiment, a tall Californian named Angela, confessed after dyeing her hair and changing her speech patterns that she, Angela, was in fact Emily; she had discovered herself and loved her new self feverishly. Emily had changed addresses five times since that incident and was still not altogether certain that she-who-had-been-Angela would not suddenly show up, hungry to assimilate her completely.

Now Emily and her Character, the one uncertain of the other, shared an apartment of reasonable size and reasonable rent. She was thinking about writing a book, which seemed as fair a thing to do as any while between lovers and not altogether enjoying spending close time with her dubious Character, shaped or no. Unfortunately the subject of the book was elusive, and long walks and a number of bottles of wine were passed in search of it. The only immediate result of these researches was a sore throat, which stayed so long past its welcome that Emily took the unusual step of seeing a doctor.

After over an hour of fruitlessly pondering the origin of the phrase *cooling your heels* in the waiting room, punctuated occasionally by semi-interesting guesses at the afflictions and complaints of her fellow heel-coolers (the woman with the knife-like nose and paper-back thriller almost certainly a chronic insomniac, or else an *invalide imaginaire*; the very young man overfond of fondling his ears probably inventing an aural fixation; but almost impossible to guess what the man trying not to look as large and out of place as he was, while actually reading an article or recipe from a dated issue of *Good Housekeeping*), Emily was led to an empty room where she could wait another fifteen minutes in privacy. She had nothing against doctors, or even dentists for that matter, but she was developing an antipathy to ceremony, and the clinic stank of it. For this reason she paid little attention to the smalltalk and thinning hair of the doctor who pleasantly squinted down her throat, shaking a tiny flashlight at her like a fetish. He applied the stethoscope, flourished the tongue depressor. He nodded at everything she said, and repeated a few phrases that had special meaning, before suggesting that he might prescribe her a little something, and then, with another nod, he left the room.

Only a few minutes later a completely different man with the same appurtenances stepped in and sat down. The moment he crossed the threshold he began talking, even before his eyes set on Emily: "Good afternoon, ah, please don't worry. You see, I am a doctor, Doctor Yam, spelled just as it sounds, but the individual who was just here is in fact not a doctor. Although he does, ah, have other notions about that."

Doctor Yam's face looked like it was made of pudding, a lighter shade of butterscotch, and he clearly enjoyed smiling close-mouthed. His hands stayed very close to one another but never touched, as though he were playing with invisible magnets, enjoying the resistance opposite poles carelessly exert.

"I hope it's not inconvenient," he shrugged, in a manner suggesting that he did not care all that much whether it was or wasn't, "but you see, ah, we're all for various sorts of semi-experimental therapies here. Nothing really wacko, mind you. If it's harmless we tend to encourage it, you know, a little exploration of this or that minor delusion, a little, ah, role-playing as the case may be. So you see ...”

“He thinks he is a doctor?”

He squeezed his nose for a full ten seconds, as if checking something, and then nodded. “Yes, I’m glad you aren’t upset, some people do get upset, unnecessarily upset. Reynolds likes to think he is a doctor. Not, you notice, that he simply *thinks he is a doctor*, but what I said is correct: he *enjoys the notion* that he is a doctor. We are still trying to work out whether he, ah, actually likes doctors at all.”

Emily tried not to look as interested as she suddenly felt. “But he’s not a doctor.”

“No, not at all,” he said, now with his eyes fully upon her but with the clear and frank wonder whether she might be an idiot. His voice assumed an even more pedantic strain: “Reynolds has never in his life shown even the slightest interest in, say, studying medicine. Until he came into my care he had been to a hospital only twice in his life.”

Emily frowned, trying to figure out whether this was interesting or not at the same time she was trying to formulate a cogent response. Indignation did not occur to her; frank curiosity would be somehow out of place. She blinked and realized that Doctor Yam had asked her a question. When she did not reply irritation forced his hands almost to press against each other. He repeated the words “sore throat.”

“But could he be one?” Emily stood up slowly. “Doctor Reynolds. Have you told him he isn’t one?”

Doctor Yam’s snort sounded like a small bird passing wind. “That would, ah, ah, defeat the purpose, wouldn’t it, of the therapeutic strategy we have adopted in *Mister* Reynolds’ case. We hope to make it apparent to him, without having to tell him, you see, that he is a, that he is not a doctor at all, for him to come to this recognition on his own.” Looking uneasy at Emily’s standing there, he also stood and set aside the clipboard in his hand for the first time that day. “This is important. Why, did you, when you were with him here just now, did you let him think he was not a doctor? Did you give

90

him the impression that he was not a doctor?"

"No, of course not. Wait, no. How could I do that?"

"Perhaps you were not an altogether convincing patient. Perhaps you, ah, did not conform to the customary program of a consultation. You are not doing so now. I notice that you evade my questions about your alleged sore throat, for example, now don't get upset, it's too late for that. So." Doctor Yam seized his clipboard to his armpit. "So." The second time around the word was a little louder, a little more rounded, and clearly final: with it, Doctor Yam impatiently whisked out of the room.

It took Emily the time a shoplifter needs to make an audacious career move to fathom that she had been – well, what would be the word? – jilted by a physician. She looked around the room once again, as though reassessing her previous, cursory measurements of its sterility, and decided to take the bright idea that everybody else seemed to be having and get out of it; a subsequent and more precise course of action, though one made with less clear and definite logic, was to pursue the faux-physician, Reynolds. Emily walked past a pair of indifferent secretarial-looking women, looking at each of the doors she passed, noting only how each madly resembled the one beside it. She used her ears instead, and sought the sound of that voice, the voice she had not really paid any attention to when it was talking to her. She tried to think of the most functionary, doctor-like voice she could imagine and listened for it, cancelling out even the sweet chirping of the nurse now following her, asking her if she could help her. From another examination room, its door not quite fully shut, the mildest voice came asking how long, how painful, all of the questions whose intimacy is removed by that mildness. Emily pushed wide the door.

Her questions to Reynolds did not come out coherently, and as she saw him return her gaze with absolutely professional sympathy, recognized the shirtless patient behind him as the *Good Housekeeping* guy from the waiting room, and felt the hand of the nurse firmly on her shoulder, confusion overtook her and she complacently wandered out of the clinic. She stopped to buy a chocolate bar on the way home and chewed it slowly. At the last bite she realized, with a sugary giggle, that what she had glimpsed on the large patient's bared chest bore an uncanny resemblance in shape to the Iberian Peninsula.

3

Scrow had no religion but he knew the words. His upbringing, when he chose to reflect on it, had been a gamut of church functions, an alternating series of prayers and potato salads. The inundation had produced a marvelous inurement. It would be hard to describe the muted joy this immunity provided: if Scrow had assimilated the metaphorical vocabulary of a science fiction buff, he might have compared his experience to that of the standard character who can stop time, freeze the motion and activities of all the things and people around him or her and derive whatever pleasures, however mild or perverse, from the unresponsive world. Scrow had no religion and was, he felt absolutely assured, somehow freer than those who did. He did, however, have a couple of barely visible stigmata: he retained a weak spot for many kinds of hymns and gospel numbers, and when, once upon a midnight, a girlfriend had initiated some action on a picnic table, he had been too amazed to be embarrassed to find himself unable to oblige.

Guilt was not much of a player in his emotional orchestra, or at least it never seemed to be – it was getting downright aggravating trying to figure out why he should have a psychosomatic whatsit. In fact, he was beginning to wonder if maybe that Yam was not a real doctor; that maybe Reynolds with his prescribed cream (Yam had looked at the scribbled note and bubbled, "Excellent, excellent," and pocketed it) was the genuine article and – oh, how he wished –

Lately in his dreams he could hear voices he knew were those of the portraits, calling him. This had him at what he thought of as Worried (which was measurably more than Rattled and even Antsy but not quite Freaking Out), especially that distinction: not the voices of the subjects of the portraits but the voices of the portraits themselves, a little choked by oil and years of silence.

He only got to Freaking Out a few minutes after he showed up for work one rainy Thursday evening and was assigned a new partner. The new partner was a talker, and liked to alternate between pseudo-jokes about how easy the job was and quasi-serious hints that he and Scrow ought not to speak too loudly or foolishly about how easy the job was, for fear of being observed by the new video system and fired on the say-so of whatever shadowy men watched the replays and undoubtedly had the power to read lips even if the new video system had no sound recording capability.

"You never know," said the new partner, a favourite expression of his. "I used to guard this place that made lightbulbs, you know, lightbulbs, how many security guards does it take to screw in a lightbulb?" A cough like wet wood splintering was his chortle. "So I used to do nights there, and sometimes I counted the lightbulbs, tried to figure out how many were there, how many might get made in a day. You know, you gotta keep thinking, think about something. You can't always be thinking about getting laid." The new partner digressed for a period on this last subject, which he did think about as much as about anything, as the two of them approached the end of the round they shared and at which point they would separate for about two hours. "You can't think about it all the time. Or anything, that's what I'm saying, you never know what'll push you over the edge. I had to get out of that job I was telling you about because I was counting lightbulbs all the time, walking into rooms and stores and restaurants and first thing I was counting up the lightbulbs in the place. Thinking too much about stuff it'll do you in, you know, you never know what. Like your looney Lemieux." Scrow blinked for clarification; no further sign was required. "Checked himself into a hospital, said he wasn't sleeping. Exhaustion, that's what they call it, but you know I heard about it, I heard he said he could hear the paintings here talking." The new partner clapped his hands. "Now that's good. I counted but I never heard lightbulbs talk! – you never know, you never know. See you back here in two."

Scrow headed on his own towards the portraits, refusing to give any look to the cameras, genuinely Freaking Out. He had never felt one way or the other about Lemieux but his almost bovine indifference to his surroundings and his supremely languid manner (which was altogether too laborious, too active a phrase to capture his essence) had seemed at least a stolid sort of sanity. Even thinking obliquely about Lemieux, or talking lightbulbs, or his own newly questionable sanity between those two ideas, made his chest flare with bright irritation – he imagined that if he unbuttoned his shirt a brutal light would burst forth, blinding anyone who might be nearby. This sensation was technically just short of Freaking Out but had no official designation at this time.

4

I could tell you that Emily Venture and Lawrence Scrow later met in that waiting room, or in the art gallery, or even that Lemieux turned out to be a mutual acquaintance and introduced them in front of a portrait of Arthur Wellesley. There's symmetry in such things, but symmetry is not an explanation – it is the opposite of an explanation. "Symmetry is our eyes fooling one another," says Doctor Yam, his fingers pressed against one another, "and what's more, fooling our minds. We, ah, see what we would prefer not to think." For a moment he is so still, so posed, that he looks like a portrait, but then Doctor (Duke) Yam stands up and slowly turns to his charts. "Excellent, excellent." The wind favours him today.

But his opponent in this re-enactment, a self-fashioned emperor named Duster, naked but for his crown, can see Doctor Yam's charts well enough, for he has his unblinking electronic eyes everywhere. There is a balm in Gilead. History will change today. And you and Emily and Scrow may dream of one another – alone, together, and real.

# THE BIGGER PICTURE

If His Excellency is not regularly pinched, and regularly here means at least one hard, full pinch in a sensitive area per hour and preferably more, there are dependably dire consequences. Many of you no doubt remember, for example, the crushing Turnip Tax of years past, only very gradually repealed after one of our most outstanding graduates boldly experimented with strategic biting. For those of you too young to recall this period, suffice it to say that executive legislation simultaneously taxed those who demonstrably possessed turnips and, even more exactingly, those who did not, with the cutting proviso that turnips were defined as anything that seemed like a turnip to His Excellency. Wisdom and justice, undoubtedly, but of a severe sort that you may help us all avoid. Wisdom and justice are not, at least not directly, your province, but if you like you may think of them as analogous to your own watchwords. Those are, I need hardly remind you, *timing and proportion*. These are the words emblazoned on the sashes you have earned the right to wear after these many years; these are the words inscribed in

the hearts of all of those who have gone before you for the past eight
centuries of His Excellency's reign; these are the words by which you
will ever be measured and celebrated, however silently.

All of this you know. And you know that my role here today is,
as this gown and sash make plain, ceremonial; that I shall endeavour
to encourage you to pinch, pinch, pinch His Excellency with timing
and proportion, as stalwartly as those eight centuries of predecessors, as
even and perhaps especially those who made the ultimate sacrifice in
the course of duty. And so I shall, and so I do . . . and yet there is more
than ceremony before us. The enormity, the vitality of your task remains,
of course, and cannot be understated. Indeed, I am about to make what
may well seem overstatements to you, but I beg you, dear graduates, hear
me.

Students being what they have always been, it is not unlikely
that many of you have before this moment heard rumours and allega-
tions to the effect that His Excellency, long may he reign over us, has in

the course of the past few decades begun to pose new challenges for our appointed pinchers. It is my duty to correct what are exaggerations, to provide you with a clear set of facts that will assist you. These facts are three. First, it is indeed true that His Excellency has taken to periodic massacres of pinchers. I hasten to add necessary historical perspective: in previous times His Excellency has himself dispatched this or that pincher, always with wisdom and justice. Before we feel too sorry for ourselves, we ought to remember the occasion just ninety years ago when an entire generation of our graduates was wiped out in the space of a single morning. There is of course no monument to those fallen, as no such structure would find purchase, let alone permanence, on the wondrous form of His Excellency, but we have our memories, our traditions, and these, these shall in your fingers be carried on and even fortified by the dangers of your task.

Second, concerning popular theories about His Excellency developing, as it were, a thicker integument: these, according to researchers, appear to have some basis in truth, and while we must certainly admire how adaptive His Excellency is, even at this remarkably cellular level, we are likewise ourselves compelled to adapt. This of course is a highly sensitive problem, in every meaning of that adjective, for while this greater skin density shall require greater force and effort in your work, I need hardly remind you, as so much of your training and concentration has been given to this consideration already, what potential dangers lie in the excess of force in any given exercise. Yes, *timing and proportion*. But this new adaptation, which may well be ongoing, means that measuring let alone knowing the valences of *timing and proportion* requires a renewed courage which I do not at all think it exaggeration to call heroic; and this heroism falls to you, to each and every one of you, even those of you who may feel you only scraped by in your studies. I assure you that our standards have never relaxed – on the contrary, if anything they have been raised, especially in the light of this new development – and not one of you has, as it were, scraped by. You are all pinchers of the highest order, with all of our faith and hopes well placed in you.

And finally to the third point, about which I speak to you precisely and only because of that placement of faith and hope just mentioned. Of the cataclysmic swattings and bashings of pinchers and even perhaps of His Excellency's remarkable growing impermeability you may have heard. But as you hear what I am about to relate, almost undoubtedly news to you all, I urge you to brace yourselves and to weigh that sash you now wear as a seal of confidence. Pinching pupils, above whose number you have now risen, must not be prematurely faced with what I now reveal all too directly to you.

We have every reason to believe that His Excellency is not, as we have always believed, the single greatest force of magnitude in existence. His Excellency is both kingdom and sovereign, and none of his wondrousness is any less wondrous today than it was ages ago, and yet I tell you that we very strongly suspect that what we have recognized as our kingdom and sovereign is neither all there is in space nor in consciousness: His Excellency, it now seems –

Please. I know this is difficult.

His Excellency, it now seems, is himself part of a greater system, a world in which he is a constituent and not the whole. But as explosive as this revelation must be to your sensibilities, there is more. Our glimpse of that greater world, though it be not more than a glimpse, finds His Excellency poised upon the surface of a being as extraordinary to Him as His Excellency appears – is – to us. This ulterior reality will strike many of you as unfathomable, blasphemous even. But again there is more: it seems very likely that His Excellency acts towards this being of such a greater magnitude conspicuously as we do towards His Excellency. Pinching, in a word.

What does all of this mean? What does the future ever mean? There is more ahead of us. And yet tradition unites us even now, as we are compelled to contemplate the disruptive unknown. We remain true to His Excellency; we shall not falter in our duty, but shall pinch, pinch, pinch; and we hold to our watchwords of *timing and proportion*, knowing that they will serve as guide and counsel as we venture into that unknown.

Tradition and adventure need not be opposed, though you have been severely taught otherwise, and it is my final duty to bid you turn and look again at those teachings, skeptically but respectfully. You have been taught that His Excellency has always been our home and will always provide, but from what I have revealed to you today will come doubts into your minds, doubts you must face and even employ with *timing and proportion*. You have been taught that there is nothing beyond His Excellency, and I have told you that we, your very teachers, no longer hold this to be certain. And you have been taught to pinch – and so you must, so you must, for is it not more important than ever that you do so? For the great fear we have always had and which we have always scrupled not to name may well be just one horror among who knows how many others, who knows how many other dangers from beyond the beyond. Our old great fear that His Excellency should relax too vigorously, even so as to shake us from the world, is now surmounted by the uncertainty of His Excellency's own stability and vigilance, an uncertainty unthinkable these past eight centuries . . .

Tradition and adventure, I have said, and it is a poor teacher who does not live by his own stated precepts. As you know, our graduation ceremonies have enjoyed a concluding tradition that sums up our commitment to economy as well as our acceptance of passing time. The valedictory address ended, the speaker, a teacher of many generations thus honoured, is trussed in his own graduation sash and thrown from what is judged the highest point of His Excellency into what was, until recently, assumed to be oblivion. And now this noble tradition may, if a somewhat personal note of triumph may be permitted, become noble adventure, in which the teacher becomes the novice student, flung into a wider and more implausible world than the one in which he awoke that morning.

I salute you, and am ready when you are.

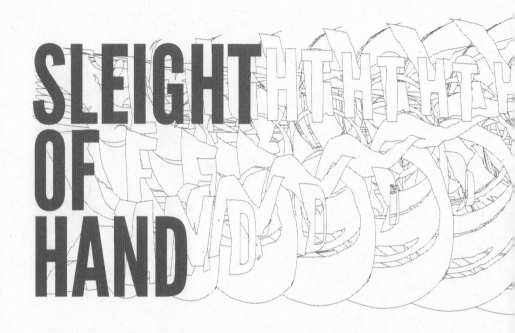

# SLEIGHT OF HAND

And since few or none prove eminently vertuous but from some advantageous Foundations in their Temper and natural Inclinations; study thyself betimes, and early find, what Nature bids thee to be, or tells thee what thou may'st be.

> — Sir Thomas Browne, *A Letter to a Friend, upon occasion of the Death of his Intimate Friend* (1690)

It was in the eighth year of our marriage that I noticed that my wife had a wooden leg. We were in a combined assault on the kitchen and I was stooped to collect crumbs when the dustpan accidentally knocked against her and the sound struck me as barky rather than fleshy, and I managed a quick, surprised but unassuming look at the item before turning to the dusting of the blinds. Not an easy subject to broach just like that: *so I see you have got yourself a* or *what on earth is* or *we haven't really had a good talk lately* or. No. So on the reliable

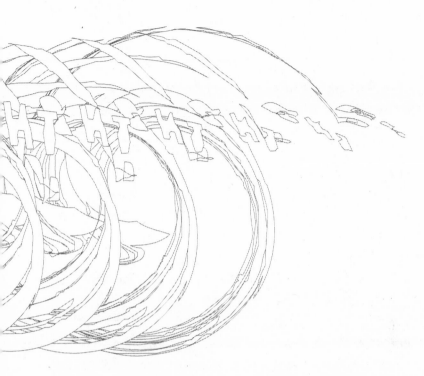

pretence of fresh air I went round to Jill's. I think that science will
one day find that the variety of endorphins is analogous to the range
of notes available to a Mozart or someone of that nature, and going
from the rigours of housecleaning to the business at hand with Jill
made for some music I think even Mozart in his illustrious career
had not managed to put together. Though I was afterwards preparing
to tell her about my discovery, she said, *I nearly forgot, there's a terrible
huge spider in the bathroom*, and pop went the opportunity and in
came a little resentment.

    The bathroom was of irregular dimensions and with subpar
lighting, so it took some time and turning about to find my object,
and I was distracted by the various objects in the room, including
miniature animal figurines, pale towels with inspirational sayings, a
cactus whose gaudy pot announced its Oaxacan origins, dozens of
gels and creams, polished cerulean tiles, no fewer than three toilet
brushes, and a sort of malfunctioning window just above the sink.

It occurred to me that I had never been in Jill's bathroom before, though that seemed preposterous; and then it occurred to me that perhaps I had been in the room before but really never taken notice of it, and as much of an insult to myself as this possibility was, it seemed both slightly more likely than that of my never having been in Jill's bathroom before and all too easily connected with my likewise somehow failing to notice that at some point my wife had adopted a wooden leg. This prospect came as a blow, or a near-blow as the case may be, because this challenge to my faculties of perception did not slow me down from looking for the *terrible huge spider*, which I now sought all the more doggedly, turning over towels and looking under the sink, as though the success of this operation might determine the question or at least assuage doubts just that little bit.

At last I saw it. No spider that, however, but a real scolopendrine horror, lurking under the soapdish at the side of the bathtub. With a pad of toilet paper I tried to crush it against the wall of the tub, but being too quick and small and lacking in seizeable dimensions, it repeatedly ran free. Then a better stratagem came to me: the merciless power of water. One swaddled hand blocked its exit up the sides while the other reached for the tap, but before I turned it a curious thing happened. The multipede, as I will call it so as to avoid spurious claims of making a firm count, halted its frenzy and turned about almost gracefully. It suggested, through a dynamic sequence of gestures too complicated to explain here, that were I to spare its life, in gratitude it would reveal to me an astonishing secret. For a few brief moments, or perhaps one long moment, I tried to guess to what that secret might pertain. Signals from the multipede insisting on the degree of astonishment to be had. I cranked the hot water tap and watched it struggle, spin, and disappear.

The image of this centripetal doom played in my thoughts when I dropped by the office. I filed some papers, moved some papers, packed up some papers to take out with me. Naturally I stopped to officially jaw with the boss and give the usual impression of the deals I was still negotiating. When there was some wondering aloud about why a certain account wasn't moving, I happened to mention that once-promising young wolf Guillory, hired only a month or two before, was not exactly keeping up with the pack, which was a shame, but added something about an illness, at which the boss, whom everyone knows washes his hands twenty times a day, turned a satisfying shade whiter and said something to the tune of *yes, well* or *as you say, a shame.* A just decent enough sort is the general opinion of the boss and as in so many such matters I am hardly inclined to dissent. Though the man has a faintly disagreeable smell that no one has been absolutely able to identify. Failed suggestions have included wet dog, burnt pumpkin, peat smoke, toast with peanut butter. The mysteries of life, I say to myself always and proceed onward, ever onward to the next.

On my way out of the office, having shuffled papers that looked good to shuffle, I ran into Dot from Personnel, who spilled a little of her hot coffee onto my wrist. This minor injury made for sustained conversation. She used to tilt her head just so back when we were you know what I mean. Don't mind if I do, said the fly to the spider. Late lunch, then, her treat because of the unfortunate the clumsy the burn beginning to assume the very shape of what island is that and we included a couple of drinks and the waiter who had a bit of sauce to him smirking when the bill came. It is useful to have useful arrangements, for example the useful room just above this establishment, perhaps she usefully remembered. Dot laughed. It was a pleasant sound until my trick knee played me a trick at an inauspicious and as it were intimate moment pressed against the wall of the useful room and Dot laughed again and what do you know but in came a little resentment. This and to some lesser extent the too-immediately postprandial vigorous exercise did not bode well for my digestion. I gallantly steered Dot back to the office without re-entering the premises myself.

It looked like rain and my watch had stopped. There are almost certainly relations between perfectly perceptible phenomena that extend beyond our plodding and workaday notions of causality, and I'm not talking about some mystical occult whatnot but deep science and explanations that so far elude us. My brother muttered all night long on his hospital deathbed and now and then could be caught his usual stuff like *never had a chance* or *no cure for life*, all of which has always exasperated me, and optimist is not the right label for the survivor who's just lucky and grateful not to have such cancer chewing at his bowels, thank you very much. He asked to be buried in his Hawaiian shirt, this same man who *never got a fair break*. Everyone had to turn the whole unkempt house upside down looking for this shirt that his wife had never seen nor heard of before, and do you know that might be the single most interesting thing he ever did. The shirt was never found, of course, though heaven and earth were moved looking for it. He was buried in a suit bought for the purpose. But imagine, a Hawaiian shirt, on this man who had never been anywhere even slightly tropical. His wife might have thought it was some sort of joke from the grave. But in any event I habitually have a disagreeable reaction to rain and so the museum's open door looked inviting enough.

Great Earthquakes of the World was the theme of the show and I leisurely took it in. One should always be open to educational possibilities, no matter the time of day. It's a funny thing, this balancing of influences: to be ever ready to let in those that make us better than we are, and to be ever ready to dam or divert those streams that pollute or else threaten to carry us away with them. Weighing this wisdom, I found myself rubbing at the burn on my wrist, which had left a mark shaped vaguely like a shark. Suddenly I thought of how horrible it would be to be devoured by a shark, and as I moved through the museum, I thought of how even more horrible it would be to be attacked by sharks in the midst of an earthquake, until I became steeled against the horror for its implausibility, a device I have always found reliable. The next hour or so was given over to the careful compiling of a list of my favourite earthquakes, ranked in order:

1. Valdivia, southern Chile, 1960: that seismic kick-ass score means enough said.
2. Shaanxi province, China, 1556: what a death toll, though no photos, of course.
3. San Francisco, 1906: more deaths caused by fire than by the quake; I never liked San Francisco.
4. Kantō region, Japan, 1923: moved the Great Buddha.

It seems doubtful that there is a sure-fire means by which to prognosticate such disasters, though I shouldn't be surprised if before long some neurographer should discover some equivalent of the Bering Strait dividing drifted regions of the brain which, if reattached, might considerably broaden human powers of under-standing even unto divination and things of that nature.

When I left the museum, besides a pleasant stimulation of the intellectual sort I enjoyed seeing the rain, for which phenom-enon I have long had a certain distaste, had abated. A newish pub a couple of blocks west gave me the opportunity to knock back a quick ale and use the telephone there to call one of the firm's on-again, off-again clients, the kind that makes a lot of bother about almost anything, and use my Guillory impression to utter such zingers as *there's only so much I can manage at this point* and *you can hardly expect me to know what the future holds.* The impression was note-perfect. I allowed myself one more ale of congratulations and made a note of the place for future reference.

My watch was still stopped but it seemed like a good enough time to head homewards, though it must be admitted that the thought of paying a visit to Ruth, buoyant Ruth, whose neighbour-hood was not far and whom I'd not seen for just over a year, did dance before me before the long hook of sober judgement yanked it away. Instead my thoughts turned to something my father had said to me when I was a very young man, perhaps all of sixteen, seventeen at most. I have no idea why I should think of it just at this moment, for the exchange was never of any importance and my father had never, to my fairly certain knowledge, said anything memorable in my lifetime. He worked as a safety inspector for a number of factories, about which occupation he never stated anything remotely like an opinion, but his hobby, if that's the right word, was magic, magic tricks and sleight of hand and all of that. He was abysmal at every trick he tried, but he kept on trying, and my brother admired him for it, while my mother tried to, and I merely refrained from hating him. He had tried to show me, on this occasion, some sort of conjuring trick with an egg, probably involving making it disappear and reappear, and I recall being worried that this was another egg that was doomed to break, and I anticipated a little resentment coming in when the egg would doubtless splatter all over my new shoes. But the egg didn't break, and it didn't disappear, but instead it hovered in the air in a really unreasonable fashion, just above my father's hands, which were gloved because he thought magicians' hands should be, and it was clear from the ridiculous look on his face that this wasn't the trick he was aiming to do, that in fact he had no idea how this was happening, and even that he was alarmed by what was going on. Gently he took up the egg in his silly gloves and looked at it quickly and then across the room, where his guide books sat open, and then at me, and he said, quietly and nervously, *no one will believe that, but you saw it*, and to the best of my ability I emptied my face and bearing of all expression. I left home not very long after that, if I'm not mistaken.

This unsatisfying reverie was halted by the sudden need to catch a driverless car that was rolling backwards into the road, not a block away from my destination. This vehicle belonged to Mrs. Halkes, an old woman whose declining capacity to drive many residents in the area had lately remarked upon. Another fellow came across the street to help me roll the aged thing back to its driveway, and held it there as I banged loudly and repeatedly at Mrs. Halkes's door. I had to introduce myself to her as I had done eight or nine times in the past year or so, without, it is honest to note, the slightest resentment, for age is what age is, and patience might be rewarded after all, and thereafter I explained to her that she must have improperly parked the car. In clear voice and terms I recommended the use of *the parking brake, also known as the emergency brake*. She blank a look me gave. It is a wonder that the dear woman hasn't burned down the house while ironing her socks. The mysteries of life, like I said.

Fatigue! And with it the need for sympathy, as I rubbed again the shark on my wrist. Therein would have to lie a tale of some description. Till then, a pickle would do nicely. I have always taken comfort in pickles, and esteem pickling as one of the finest, most ingenious, and most enduring of human inventions, superior to, for example, the sewing machine, ballet, the paperclip, the pogo stick, and silverware. I made my way in quietly and ignored the credit card bill on the sideboard. The kitchen was a wonder to behold, tidied and then some, all surfaces uncluttered, nary a smear nor a smudge, everything in its place and a place for you get the idea, clean, cleaner, cleanest.

# LEGACY

When the old Duchess coughed, which she often did without warning, it was a convulsive cough, a full-body affair, *hhhrrk-kkkklllkkkh*, which everyone in the vast house could hear, all the way upstairs and all the way downstairs, and after everyone halted to hear it out, *hhhhhrrrkkkjklllk*, she would with the next peaceful breath vehemently declare, "I'm still here." Whether she was shaking the dinner table with her coughing, *hhhrrkkhrrkkkhrk*, or suddenly thrashing on her bed pillows, *hhrhrrjrjrkkkkrrrhhh*, everyone stopped, family or servants or hangers-on, eyes wide, until she gave the unfailing signal, never an exclamation as such but a crisply pronounced sentence with a full-stop, "I'm still here." The cue would halt before the ball, the knitting needles cross and stick together, the laden fork hover as the coughing overtook her, *hhhrrrkjkkkhrrr*, as she coughed and coughed, *hrrrjrrjrrkkklllh*, at any given moment, for the necessary duration, invariably concluded with the defiant sentence, loud and clear for everyone to hear, "I'm

still here." Time's passing could be felt if not exactly measured in this irregular way, as though time came in jerking fits like the old Duchess's terrible coughs, *hrrrkkkkkllllkkhhrrk* and *hrrrhrrjrrkkllhhrrk* or in eyes widening and narrowing again, like the eyes of the family and the servants and the hangers-on, with the toll ringing reliably in the sentence, "I'm still here," reminding everyone that there is still time, that time is still passing. And as time passed, and the ancient Duchess coughed and coughed, *hhhrhrrrrkkkhrrrkkkhrrkk*, coughing as it were for dear life, *hrrhrrkjrjrkkrrrlllhrrkkh*, there were fewer and fewer family members and servants and hangers-on to suspend or at least slow their activities, widen those eyes still inclined to do so, and wait through the coughing and coughing, *hhhhhrrjrrrkkkjrrk-kkkhrrrllllkkk*, to see whether the same voice would proclaim, "I'm still here," and it did, it always did, until eventually she violently coughed and coughed, *hrrrkkkllllkkhrrrrjrrkkllhhrrk*, and there was no one waiting, there was no one to assure with the nonetheless clearly enunciated announcement, "I'm still here." It would surely be instructive to know what was the last human sound in that mighty house before, after such a long span of neglect, it fell in on itself and dissolved into memoryless rubble: that relentless cough or those inexorable words.

# THE ALARM CLOCK

Shortly after Ilya and I moved into the new house we bought a new alarm clock. The radio dial on my old clock had become jammed, and frustrated attempts at tuning found only midpoints between stations. This new clock, sleek and black and cubic, projected large green numerals in the darkness, where its dusty brown predecessor, which I had had for over a dozen years, including my student days, shone red, somehow less urgent numbers.

One afternoon, a few days after the new clock assumed its place as the bed's witness at the corner of my dresser, I found myself looking for the old alarm clock. I am not sure why, but suddenly I wanted it again, and could not remember whether I had thrown it out. After some little searching in different rooms I asked Ilya, as casually as possible, if she had tossed it in the trash or ...? Ilya is quite amazing for the earnest thought she almost always puts into answering such mundane, unimportant questions, but this once I had hoped she would not give it much thought. She wasn't sure, she

said, and then quickly added: *why?* Maybe she is accustomed to my unimportant questions being irrationally important, I don't know; but it occurred to me that she probably *had* thrown away the old clock and, perhaps not even truly being sure herself that she had in fact done so, was worried that now I had some need of it, a need she could not have foreseen because it was as irrational as most of my ridiculous behaviour, and so said she wasn't sure because she was worried I might be upset, possibly even upset at her, if I did have such a need now, and she wanted to gauge how important this particular matter might be, how upset I might potentially become. She usually overestimates this potential, but I hope that fact merely speaks well of her and not ill of me.

No reason, just wondering, I answered, and then continued the search. I tried the guest room, where only recently we had had a couple of guests staying, some friends of Ilya's, and it occurred to me that Ilya might have placed the old clock there for them to use.

The notion of one or both of those friends accidentally taking the clock, which was too large to be accidentally taken up or packed, vanished almost as quickly as it first appeared, to be followed by conjectures about whether one or both of them might have deliberately taken it, which my reasonable inner voice at once dismissed and then shortly afterwards I did, too. I tried the linen closet, carefully checking between each layer of folded towels and bedsheets, and then made such a mess I had to refold half of the contents and completely rebuild the pile. With each fruitless minute of searching that passed, I felt I could visualize the old clock that much more vividly. Not just see it, but recall the touch of it, the minimal solidity with which it reacted to my smacking of, and sometimes blindly around, the snooze button, and then gradually what seemed to be the entire history of this object with me – *our relationship* is probably too strong a phrase – began to replay in my thoughts.

All of the times I had been late for important appointments or trivial engagements lived again, though now of course drained of all of their anxiety and retouched, here or there, with bright humour. The horror of seeing 8:55 rather than, say, 7:55, had become the endearing stuff of farce. Not a few notes of remembered lust sounded, of encounters by the lights of 12:17, 2:20, and – in from a sudden rainstorm, soaked and wine-lipped – 3:46. Certain arrangements of certain digits appeared in my mind, like dutiful acrobats assuming one shape after another, all angles perpendicular by design. 11:10, yes! 4:04, yes, palindromically, yes! How I had lived at 5:38 – yes, yes, again yes!

But no, I could not find it, not even after Ilya had gone out to get some groceries and I, no longer forced to be furtive about it, became aggressive in the search, even looking into the attic where neither of us had ever packed anything. It had occurred to me that Ilya might have hidden the clock, for reasons I could not imagine but did not worry about, and I took to poking in obscure corners and drawers. The laundry room took nearly an hour to check thoroughly, not least because I was trying to imagine myself a sneaky Ilya, a possessed Ilya, an upset Ilya. Where to stash the alarm clock, and thereby eliminate my past, my history before her? This was a totalitarian Ilya, one I could have glimpsed, if only I had been more alert, many times before this moment: examples big and small, major and minor herded into my thoughts. When asked whether the clock had gone in the trash, she had evaded answering. She had asked *why?* and shown, it might have been, suspicion, distrust. If I found the old clock – wedged between the dryer and the washing machine? buried in paint rags? behind the furnace? – I might be stuck in the past. Worse yet (I imagined her thinking to herself), the cheap thing might serve as a kind of *time machine* (Ilya has never had much interest or even patience in science fiction, and so probably grimaced at the phrase), a vehicle by which I might either return myself to a past world and past life, one without a mortgage and leaf-clogged drainpipes and weekend newspaper delivery or, no less unlikely, return us both to earlier times in our coming together, maybe problem times, revisiting troubles and arguments and sadnesses that ought to be finished. This is (thinks Ilya, in the most totalitarian sort of pronouncement I can imagine her making) the Era of the Green Numbers; history is junk.

Junk, that's the other option: that she has indeed thrown it out. Just the thought made me want a pint of beer, even though beer had not been my usual fare for some time. I couldn't remember the last time I was in a pub with a pint of beer, something I used to enjoy; but those days belong to the Era of the Red Numbers. I was resistant to this declaration, which was uttered by a strange voice, a combination of my own and a poor imitation of Ilya's. Just saying it, just thinking it, did not make it true.

That's how I found myself in a pub that none of my friends, even the most devil-may-care or the seediest, would have bothered to visit. If it had a name, it was nowhere visible. Smoking had been outlawed a few years before but the smell was still in residence (in fact, I thought I saw an ashtray or two). My table had slight gouges in its surface, the chair a lump, but the pint of beer was fine and I was thinking: just saying something, just thinking something, does not make that something true – because you can always say or think the exact opposite immediately afterwards. It is not true because it cannot be true.

To get myself out of this empty spin cycle of quasi-thinking, I looked around the place and eventually settled my attentions on the pinball game in the corner. It announced itself in fiery hues: BLASTOFF! The contraption was probably a decade older than I was, but seemed to function, even if nobody else was paying it the slightest attention. After a few more mouthfuls of beer, I approached the bartender and asked him for some change so I could play. He gave a wet cough over his shoulder while he rang the register open. The man's hairstyle had not changed since 1955, though he himself looked younger than that. A comb poked out of his front pocket, I remember, and his watch was an analog. When he dropped the quarters into my hand he wished me *good luck*.

Pinball is a remarkably uninteresting game and I have always been confused not by the players of such games but by the spectators. No sooner had I drawn back the firing pin to launch the first ball of the game than somebody brought his drink over and leaned nearby to watch. Peripherally I noticed his fingered beard, his toothy half-grin, and a pair of shabby sandals. He said nothing as I paddled the ball into the DANGER ZONE a couple of times, winning 250-point bonuses without much effort, forcing a few rings out of the old thing and even a stray buzzer, the happy fart of a long-constipated old geezer, alerting us to the double-score METEOR SHOWER I had apparently navigated with commendable success. The ball sprang up near the UNKNOWN PLANET and was caught in a side loop that ruthlessly tracked it down and out of my control. With the next ball, I quickly doubled the score again and bounced off HALLEY's COMET for an 800-point whistle, when my hard left flipper batted it up again towards the UNKNOWN PLANET and again it was sucked into what I then saw was labelled as a GRAVITY WELL and pulled out of play.

At this point the spectator spoke. In a low grumble he said:

*The Unknown Planet is a bitch.* I turned to give a weak smile more as
a sign of agreement than as any encouragement to further conversation, which I was in no mood to have, but in his face I discovered
a look of such severity that the smile never happened, never even
started. Now his full figure was in view, and it would be hard to say
what was the more fantastic: his dress, which was for all one could
see a kind of dirty djellaba, or his height, for he was easily six feet tall
while slouching. At some point in this very short exchange between
us his hand gripped my shoulder, though when he put it there I
couldn't say, and when he spoke again it was in an even lower tone
than before, as though to ensure no one might overhear. When he
finished speaking, he gave me a fierce nod, took a slow look around
the pub like an animal on the watch for predators, and slipped out
the front door.

    Anger – or at least irritation – must have been my first reac-
tion. I took a generous gulp of beer and massaged my hands. I fired
the third and final ball as hard as I could, guiding it through THE
DOUBTFUL NEBULA to strike repeatedly between the BINARY STARS
bumpers, a nervous pulse of 200 points, 200 points, 200 points.
The ball descended fast but my flipper caught the edge of it and
dispatched it into the DANGER ZONE, thence back to the BINARY
STARS and to the brightly illuminated COSMIC RAYS, which progress
set the old machine flashing and bleeping and tooting with excitement, the points rolling in, the red digits barely solidifying before
being forced to present others, and I again pounded the ball with
just enough force up, up towards the UNKNOWN PLANET and its
untold promise of high scoring, smoothly bypassing the GRAVITY
WELL but just shy of the UNKNOWN PLANET itself, ringing some
inferior heavenly body's bell. Down again rolled the ball to the
defensive, twitching flippers. A full and satisfying smack promptly
returned it to the region of the UNKNOWN PLANET but this time the
GRAVITY WELL had its way, and the words GAME OVER flashed above
my five-figure score.

    After the rest of my quarters were spent, I returned to the

bartender for another pint and more change. Once more he wished me *good luck*. Restraining an undignified snort, I asked if he knew the very tall man who had been beside me at the game. He cocked his head and looked at me with curiosity, then nodded. He offered nothing more, but the odd thing is that I didn't ask. I went back to the pinball machine, dropped in a new quarter, and thought: something can be true and its exact opposite can also be true, whether I like it or not.

I had four pints that afternoon, spent close to twenty dollars on BLASTOFF! and never once reached the UNKNOWN PLANET. When I walked home I wondered what Ilya supposed had happened to me. She has probably long been used to my erratic movements, but on the other hand she is very capable of worrying, and truth be told I have probably given her cause to worry more than once. During that evening walk, the worst scenarios began to take shape: home with the groceries, Ilya discovered my absence as well as definite signs of wild searching in the house. She has concluded that I've been abducted (but there is no evidence of any struggle); or that I've discovered some secret of hers, like a concealed diary detailing scads of infidelities, and decided to go (though strangely without taking a single thing with me besides my wallet); or that I've actually found my old alarm clock and, having discovered its true nature as a time machine, have been propelled back in time (and this possibility, I found it sobering to discover, was the one with the least ready counterevidence). Ilya has gone to the authorities, has succumbed to panic or despair, has already started a new life with someone else, perhaps one of the names in the diary.

I walked no faster out of fear of what I might discover. Here I was returning from voyages into the past (a past of beer-drinking, of other lovers), into the future (a future of fantastic interstellar travel), come to face the question of what effects my actions yielded in the so-called continuum of my life with Ilya. Our neighbourhood looked the same, but a stout child in an inside-out shirt standing pointlessly on a corner seemed unfamiliar. I walked no faster, though naturally my behaviour struck me as ridiculous: how could my walking home this fast or this slow affect anything? The stout child in the inside-out shirt had an ambiguous stare.

Without knowing why, I stopped next to the child and looked across and down the street at the house Ilya and I had bought a little over a year before. It was a good house and it was good to live in it. The neighbourhood was good and I was even willing to give this unknown child the benefit of the doubt. Without taking my eyes from the house, I said: *It was a cheap, old alarm clock and the radio dial on it was jammed. I don't really mind that it's gone. It's just a symptom of a deeper anxiety, one that's really troubling my day-to-day life. The problem is that I want to be definite about everything but I don't want everything to be definite.*

And the expressionless child looked at the house, the house where Ilya and I lived, for a few moments, before turning in the opposite direction and unhurriedly walking away, into the future.

# TALES TOLD BY AN IDIOM

In a small agrarian town in northern Quebec, they have a saying: *le voisin n'a qu'une maison*, "the neighbour has only one house" or "the neighbour only has a house," depending on where one prefers to hear the emphasis. Exactly what this phrase means has proved a puzzle for linguists and sociologists. Though not altogether inhospitable, the steely-eyed townsfolk do not much care for the questions of outsiders. Suggestions of an unknown story behind the expression – of its being a mnemonic tag (of no known specific use), of its being part of an allegory or homily (perhaps distorted by abbreviation, the way "the proof of the pudding is in the eating" has disintegrated to the incoherent "the proof is in the pudding"), or of its having some historical basis (an account of a specific someone's neighbour, maybe, or a particular house) – all remain unverified. Unfortunately, it has not even been determined whether the following scenarios are accounts of real incidents or inventions produced for the very purpose of illustration, but they are faithfully recorded here as they

were found, received, or told, with as much detail and context as were available.

After a long rainstorm, a man out walking is struck by a large, sodden branch that breaks off from a very old tree and pins him to the ground. Two sawyers working nearby rush to his aid and he informs them that he is barely able to breathe; they must hurry. But the branch is too heavy for them to lift. The first sawyer offers to run and fetch a saw, not sixty paces away, but the second sawyer becomes concerned that the pinned man might die in the interim, and while the first sawyer would be subsequently commended for his fast thinking and valiant efforts, the second sawyer would look like a dolt waiting and helplessly watching the man die, and so the second sawyer tersely accuses the first sawyer of not lifting his part of the branch with all of his apparently little strength. So the sawyers again try to lift the branch, and ultimately collapse with even more huffing and panting than before. The pinned man signals that he is without air. The second sawyer announces that he will fetch the saw, and the first sawyer, seeing what his unscrupulous partner is playing at, promptly socks him in the jaw. The second sawyer gets up from the ground and rushes headlong into the first, the two of them crashing together into the tree. This impact causes another branch to break off, and it bounces off of one end of the first fallen branch, neatly knocking it off the gasping man, who crawls toward the other people who have now gathered at the scene. The two sawyers have hit each other half a dozen more times before they realize what has happened. A witty bystander might aptly remark: *le voisin n'a qu'une maison.*

Children play in such tall grass that they cannot see one another. They soon become separated but, each thinking that the others must be together, none wants to be the first to cry out for help, and thus the first branded a coward and surely taunted ever after. One finally has the ingenuity to call out accusing another of being lost. Years later, the friends recount this story at a reunion and own up to their common fears, but they cannot agree which of them came up with the solution. Angrily the inspired one leaves the party, muttering, *c'est vrai que le voisin n'a qu'une maison.*

Making summer afternoon love by a stream, a young couple is interrupted by cries for help, but they cannot see who is calling and cannot bring themselves to break their exquisite rhythm. The voice shouts that it is drowning, drowning, drowning, but neither lover can see anyone in the unconcernedly flowing water, and their ardour won't let them part. By the time they are sated, the cries have stopped. They explore the area, and walk downstream a good mile or more before they give up. When they say goodbye to one another, each seems embarrassed and uncertain. Each attends closely to the local news and town talk for days afterward, but neither finds any report of any drowning, and the absence of any such report stymies their communications with one another. They can speak of nothing else, but of this subject they have nothing to say. She changes her hair, and he silently judges the style wrong. He is offered a new job in the next town, a town the two of them had habitually remarked upon as an undesirable place to live, and she tries to be encouraging. After he has moved and eventually finds that the job and the town both suit him, he writes a letter to his friend and tells him about the incident that summer afternoon, and reflects on how fickle the heart is. His friend's reply: "You idiot, *le voisin n'a qu'une maison*."

A father accuses his son of stealing his boots, and the offended son leaves home. In a distant town he finds work as an assistant to a rheumatic sawbones, a kindly man who recognizes the young man's talent for swift and acute diagnosis, and begins to teach him about more than the ordinary ailments and tried and sometimes true remedies. The young man devotes himself to medicine and becomes so trusted by the local people that he very gradually takes over the old doctor's practice. Within a few years he finds himself brought in to deliver the mayor's child, a difficult operation because the woman's cervix is, like her husband, anything but flexible, and the labour lasts three days. On the morning of the third, a message is brought to the physician: it is from his father, who reports that he has found his boots, and all is forgiven. The mayor's wife pauses in her shrieking when she sees her doctor's face momentarily lose its imperturbable aspect, and asks him what is wrong. He answers, *le voisin n'a qu'une maison*, and resumes his work.

Complaining of his breakfast at an inn, a guest unconsciously runs his fingers through his beard as he is dressing down the manager, a woman who takes this gesture as a lewd suggestion. She takes greater offence than she might because, sordid truth be told, she was feverishly fantasizing about this very guest's beard the night before, which is not at all the sort of thing she would normally do. She more than matches his barrage of insults. Not accustomed to hoteliers abusing him, and surprised and upset to hear that his beard-stroking was in any way vulgar, the guest begins stammering an apology, whereupon the manager, realizing that she has overdone it, herself begins to apologize. She says that his dinner will be on the house, and he replies that he will only accept if she will dine with him. Just then the manager's miserable, lazy, and clean-shaven husband, who has just been stealthily coming down the staircase behind them, snarls *le voisin n'a qu'une maison*, but chokes on the last word, and rolls down the remaining stairs to the floor, never to be revived. On his headstone his widow has written: *le voisin n'a qu'une maison*.

An unmarried schoolteacher arouses the distrust of a student's mother, who thinks that such situations are ghastly beyond words. This mother circulates the story that the schoolteacher is known to walk the streets at night, perhaps asleep but perhaps not, and the story's vagueness ensures that it spreads like wildfire in a high wind. The schoolteacher finds herself unwelcome in certain places and unacknowledged by certain people. One day she overhears two of her students recounting a version of the story, and she decides to take up walking the streets at night, but dressed in her mother's bridal gown. The story evolves and diversifies in quick response to witness accounts of her wordless, almost ethereal perambulations: she is a widow, longing for her dead husband, in love with a ghost; she has been seduced by some man in the community, who will not do right by her, perhaps because he is already married, and these nightly marches are her mute but moving protest; she is a lunatic, imagines herself wed to the moon; she has been hypnotized by the wicked schoolchildren, and unknowingly seeks a groom every night; she is holy; she is cursed; she is the picture of sorrow; she is a sign of hope. The mother's original story and spite are eclipsed. Without exception her students all become more attentive to their studies. One cloudless night a man walks out to intercept her in the middle of the street, falls to his knees and asks for her hand in marriage. She says with a voice not her own, *le voisin n'a qu'une maison*.

126

A man loses his boot walking through an extremely muddy field one rainy evening. He arrives home and his father-in-law, with whom the man, his wife, and their children live, asks him what inspired him to go out in such weather in one boot. Trying to assume the patience necessary for dealing with this suspicious, narrow-minded old goat, the man explains that on the eve of the feast of St. Bunions it is considered good luck to walk in the evening with only one boot. His father-in-law scoffs but is still thinking about it when he retires to his room. He wonders whether there is some truth to the story, or whether it is simply some excuse meant to conceal something, and his inability to decide between these possibilities sends him out later that night, when the others are asleep in bed, in one boot, determined to find out which is the case. In the now quite fierce wind and the rain he hobbles and anxiously looks about, without having any set idea as to what he is looking for, and before long he is completely lost, though he does not admit as much to himself, and keeps hunting for his answer. He is found, shivering in a small wood, early the next morning. A doctor asks him some questions as he examines the old man sleepless in his bed, but obtains only nonsensical answers about hidden treasure, his many enemies, a saint nobody has heard of. The doctor is asked by one of the children whether grandfather will be all right, and he answers, "It is difficult to say, but *le voisin n'a qu'une maison.*"

A daring fox has been attacking a number of adjacent poultry farms, inspiring wagers in a popular tavern as to who is to be the next victim. One evening, when the betting is high and the laughter loud, the odds-on favourite, a grizzled and gruff man to whom life has seldom been kind, loses his composure and openly sobs into his drink. Early the next morning, the fox is killed by hunters and its carcass is brought to the sad farmer. He holds it up by the tail and says, *le voisin n'a qu'une maison.* The next day he puts the farm up for sale and leaves the country.

Recounted by a nonagenarian in a Sherbrooke nursing home: "If you threw a stone in a pond, and there was this large pond near the old cottage, one of my cousins nearly drowned there, and we teased him for years afterwards, called him The Fish, there goes The Fish, he hated that. What they don't know, I'll tell you, is how long a grievance can last. And I doubt their medical credentials, I'll tell you that. But it was the pond wasn't it, to return to our subject, if you threw a stone in a pond, you would naturally expect what are they called ripples, yes, but if you threw a stone in the pond and there were absolutely no ripples, and though this has never happened to a stone I threw, and look at me, I'm not going to be throwing any stones now, but do you know, never count anybody out, I'll tell you that, never count anybody out. But that pond. Any pond, really. The trick is to throw a stone into it without causing a single ripple, and once I saw this done by a small girl nobody thought capable of anything, she was always following our gang around, and after all of us gave up on the game, she picked up a stone and threw it right in, not a single ripple. That girl went on to marry a big shot, I heard, I don't remember who told me, but what I said when I heard about it was *le voisin n'a qu'une maison*, as my grandmother used to say when she cut up the lemons. And that really summed it up, you know."

A talented singer finds herself unable to master a particular score that she has agreed to perform. The piece is not especially demanding, she admits to her mother, but invariably her breathing becomes irregular somewhere in the middle and her enunciation falters. She must impress this patron and cannot turn down the commission without injury to her reputation and career. Her mother assures her that everything will be all right, that she will surely master the piece soon, that it is probably just nerves. The daughter seethes in silence: how she wishes her mother could be more severe with her, slap her across the face and shout at her to work harder, or else be less encouraging, say to her that the commission doesn't matter, that this only shows that music was never really her future; but instead it will always be all right, according to her mother. She decides that she will disgrace herself on stage to shatter her mother's unwavering faith in her, and ceases practising for the concert. The night before the concert, however, her mother accidentally reveals that she is having an affair with her daughter's patron, and it is only as a favour to his lover that he has invited her daughter to perform. The daughter appears to applause the next evening wearing the gown her mother has bought her for this occasion and, instead of singing the advertised work, trills the words *votre voisin, n'a-t-il qu'une maison?* to the tune of a ditty she learned in childhood.

# STERNER STUFF

I freely admit, I am not a very good gravedigger. But I can't help it. I don't mean I can't help how bad I am, because as any objective observer would have to acknowledge, my work and my skill have improved over time; no, what I mean is I can't help it that I keep digging graves, it's just something I have to do. In no other respect would I be judged a compulsive person. My daily routine is no more fixed than anyone else's and there are no shrieking fits or even

shortness of breath if that routine is upset. But I'm serious about gravedigging. I think the dead should be put in the ground. I think that's very important. And sometimes I think people underestimate how important or urgent this is, and I freely admit, this upsets me, this propels me into action. What's the expression? Gets ahead of himself. Or gets ahead of the curve. I get ahead of myself.

Which is how I come to this spot of trouble, Your Honour.

# THE BAD FATHER

As you may have yourself discovered, just when the shops are closing is a terrible time in which to find a gift for a party later that evening, and this was the quandary in which Clive found himself less than an hour before he was due at his ex-wife's house. Snow was teasing the sky and effected a certain panic among the cars below, which made finding a place to park that much more of a job. A side street was tried after another side street, and after that a narrower side street, Clive muttering the unheard-of street names as curses, looking at signs, trying to look around or through obstacles. The lights of shops went out one after another.

Having parked far from those dimming commercial lights, Clive jogged the way a man who does not typically exercise in this way jogs through the side streets, turning here and there. He found a candy store with those nice lemon drops closed, a stationer's shop with fancy pens closed, a few places that might have sold something to the purpose, all closed. He had no idea what he was looking for

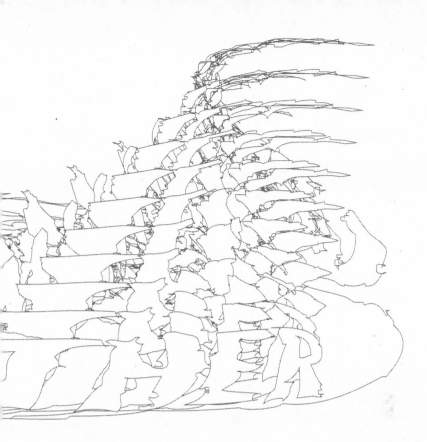

beyond the general concept of buying a gift, and he was breathing heavily when he stopped at a shop window he almost didn't spot, peered in, tried to figure out whether the place was still open.

The door pushed open but the place was dank and dark. Clive gradually made out various crowded and cobwebbed shelves and an antique cash register. Empty birdcages. Lamps, candlesticks, a row of eye-droppers. Coiled springs nestled in boxes with speckled handkerchiefs. A sextant leaning against a microscope. Jars of marbles and towers of spools. Expressionless figurines in uncertain poses. Bookends shaped like owls. A xylophone or something very like one.

The owner, if that's who it was, slowly shuffled into view from behind a curtained doorway. It might have been a man or a woman, but for that matter it might have been an animated pile of papers and dust, for so it looked. The tendered smile was made of a thousand interwoven facial creases; the voice that offered assistance rattled deep within.

Still looking round at the unpromising bric-a-brac all about him, Clive hurriedly explained the need for a suitable present for his daughter, something unique and needed immediately. "It is her tenth birthday. She is an unusual girl. She likes unusual things." As he was speaking, his gaze slipped through a pile of beaten boxes on a high shelf. He reached up to move the boxes aside, and pulled down the dull red object there. It was not a ball, as he had first thought, but a polyhedron, whose vertices were puckered with dials and its faces alternately engraved with markings and punctured with delicate little holes. Porcelain maybe, but very old. Clive held up the ball in vain hopes of seeing it in a better light, and then applied his eye to one of the holes. Flakes and tiny sticks of shifting colours coalesced into a moving shape, then into another, and another, as he could not help turning the object in his hands. Was that a woman dancing? No, now it was two men fencing, and now a proud horse leaping until it became a massive shining bird, which flew high until it burst into flame.

"What is this?" The question, he realized as he asked it, didn't matter.

"If it has a proper name," the proprietor answered with a chuckle akin to a snake's cough, "I have forgotten it. We might satis-factorily call it an amusement. It is unique, and the story goes that the master who devised this original amusement, at the behest of a potentate's child, died after its completion. Yet its history is even more singular than that."

"Great," said Clive.

"It is said that the young heir in question disappeared not very long after the amusement was given to him. It is said that he played with it for days, turning it round and round, twisting the dials, unlocking its abilities and its secrets. Nothing but it could hold his attention: he took it with him to his bed at night and began his mornings with it in his hands. But one day the servants found the amusement sitting unattended on the floor of the heir's bedchamber, and the young heir was nowhere to be found. There was speculation that the amusement had swallowed the young heir's soul."

"Sounds perfect," said Clive. He had missed – had actually forgotten – last year's birthday. Not this year.

"But beware," the gnarled face continued, and a bony finger rose before it, "if it is exposed to the light of a full moon: for these apertures will take in that luminescence and awaken a mystery best left dormant within the device. Flout it at all other times, in any weather, but on the night of a full moon wrap it in some thick cloth, store it in shadow – keep it far from the full moon's light."

"Got it," said Clive. The party was due to start in ten minutes, and it was going to take at least twice as long to get there, and he still had to get back to the car.

"We have called it an amusement for the sake of convenience, and it is an amusement, a very old and remarkable amusement, perhaps even an endlessly diverting amusement, but there are very specific conditions for how it may be given as a gift and how it is to be handled. No one else should play with it but the person to whom it is given. It is for her and her alone. Others who try to usurp it or possess it without permission may find it harmful. The amusement belongs only to whom it is given, and the amusement will resent the presumptions of others."

"Great," said Clive.

"Above all, there is one most important prohibition. The child may look through any of the apertures and delight at the visions she finds within, but not *this* aperture," and the bony finger identified the one in question, which looked no different at all from the others, "never *this* one. There are great dangers in this one."

"Great," said Clive.

"There are those who believe that play is inextricably bound up with danger, and there are those who believe this is as it should be. Of such things have I no judgement. Yet even such an ancient fool as I readily observes that some hazards can never be properly called part of play, even if play may lead one towards them."

135

"Great," said Clive. "How much?"

The proprietor did not seem to understand the question.

"How much do you want for it?"

"Oh," came the reply, "thirty-six fifty-five."

Then Clive was out into the snow, now in earnest and joined by wind, reckoning its adverse effect on his estimated time of arrival. Clutching the hastily wrapped amusement under his arm, he tried to remember whether this next corner was a left or a right. His ex-wife would have nothing so unique, nothing with such rich history to it, the magical bauble that would belong to her and to her alone, but that last corner did look familiar. He retraced his steps, already quickly filling in behind him, and then retraced those other steps. There was the shop with the cheap lemon drops, that was encouraging. He took another right. A young couple, arm in arm, passed him but their intimate laughter stopped him from asking the name of the street. He took another left. Then another.

Like a beacon, a blue light ahead shone out between the blowing streaks of white. Clive thought suddenly and stupidly of the fairy who transforms Pinocchio, and it may have been this sudden and stupid thought that prevented him from breaking into a sprint, to see the light for what it was and try to get to the truck before it towed his car out of the private lot and away, away. But it was going away by the time he was running, and he shouted as he ran, and tried to bang his arm against the side of the truck, but could not even see the driver or be sure that he was being heard. He shouted again and struck again, but the truck dragging his defeated car was away, well away.

It had not been just his arm that had struck the truck. The gift lay irreparably in pieces in the deepening snow, the torn wrapping flapping about. His eyes itched, or perhaps just the one eye, the eye that had seen the dancing woman and the duelists and the leaping horse and the shining bird and the fireball. His hands were empty and it was late.

He went to a bar, which he had no difficulty finding, and got very drunk, very nearly carelessly drunk.

Late the next day he telephoned his ex-wife and made apologies and excuses, but his daughter, the unusual girl of ten, never spoke to him again.

Has this ever happened to you?

# HEAVY LIFTING

– Do insomniacs have a lesser or greater probability of suicide? If the former, it is because they cannot bring themselves to surrender awareness; they do not want to miss even what only might happen. If the latter, it is because they cannot bring themselves to surrender awareness, though they wish and wish and wish. The distinction, if there is one, might have to do with whether the insomniac's unrelenting awareness is of the world around him or of the way in which he is aware of that world, of how he is ceaselessly turning it over, but who knows if either is more exciting, more exhausting, more masochistic.

The machine is not easy to start again when it winds down, stalls, or has been inactive for a spell. It would probably be no exaggeration to say that it resists starting. Easy does it, all the same. Always the option to call for the servicemen, but that's an ordeal unto itself. They come in pairs as a rule, in dirty boots as another rule. Coarse men, usually one of them a big talker about nothing and

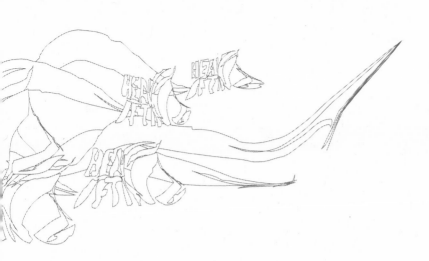

everything and the other either silent as the dead or affirming every opinion of his partner, all the while thoroughly muddying the tiles and towels. Waiting in dread for them to show up later even than would seem reasonable, and an attendant sense of desecration after they've gone. Easy does it, there it is.

– But who knows if either is more exciting, more exhausting, more masochistic.

Just think of that genie and the bottle routine: the right rub gets the wish. Tough to get, that's what the machine plays, according to the servicemen, who like to talk in this way. Picture what will happen to the carpet if they come, the two of them, not altogether unfriendly. Easy does it, but easy isn't doing it, is it? Reaching around. Changing the grip. All this ungainly ganglia of tubing. Hold it here, hold it. No nonsense now.

– The mystery may lie in the degree to which we can imagine. The sleepless mind drawing for itself an ever incomplete picture of what the next moment looks like, the moment when that mind is not there to observe it. The suicidal mind likewise trying to begin a drawing it can never begin of what the world looks like without that mind looking at it. The inspiration, if that's the word, of defying the rules of what can and cannot be observed, when and how that observation occurs.

Mind the carpet, mind the carpet! Complaining about what boots of what servicemen when not minding the mess of one's own. Amateurs, professionals, amateur messes and professional messes. It's tight all right, just hold it so. Nobody ever said machines were made to make everyone's lives easier. Exactly the sort of thing the big talker type of serviceman would observe, bound to show up and say it, and if not in those exact words, bound to show up eventually and say it in those exact words. Is that supposed to be flashing? Easy does it, let's not make a mess of the mess.

– It is not, then, just a matter of whether or not to perceive. It is a matter of the conditions of that perceiving, a dissatisfaction with the very operation of perception. And dissatisfaction is too simple, too mild a term for what may be a passion, a torment, likely as not both together.

Philosophy leaks. No matter how you tilt the whole thing. No matter how tight the adjustments. No matter what the advertisements say. Get used to the fact. Is it toxic, the stuff that leaks out? Is it poisonous, or has it curative properties? There must be some research into these things. The promise of hair restoration, instant love, invisibility. At any rate there is, no question, a detergent designed for the stains, reasonably priced. The carpet, the carpet, and the drapes.

– Why this waking state at all . . .

Pain like pain was meant to be when it was first invented. That's a pinched nerve, what comes with such a poor grip. Squeeze out of that corner. Pain pain pain. The machine doesn't care. It thinks, leaves caring out of the equation, thinks and leaks and leaves the caring and carrying and cleaning and the pain pain pain to.

Nobody ever said, yes they did. Easy now. The thing could crush bone if and when it got as excited as now.

– And there are no rhetorical questions. Why am I not sleeping? Not a rhetorical question! Why am I alive? Not a rhetorical question!

The machine can stall even when it's most excited: it just seems to hit a kind of maximum intensity and then stop. And then there's a real job, the servicemen and their remarks, the embarrassment. Takes more persuasion than. Takes a cool head a loving touch the right tool, do you get the yes. It's not even discernible in the voice. You can't trust it, the voice always assured and assuring in that grave, deep sort of way.

– Never mind whether the one who asks is alive or not. Even a recorded voice, yammering on long after perhaps all of sentient life has withered and gone, can ask such a question, and still, still it is not rhetorical; still it can never be rhetorical.

That lamp wobbling, watch it, an heirloom. Ever so much as a peep at the manual? Fourteen registered kinds of solipsism. And a couple of them are, try to get this, infectious, now there's technology gone mad for you, right there in the vocabulary. Easy, use the knees, such as they are. And as if on fucking cue. No, think about anything else about the itch, about scratching the knee you can't reach.

– But: am I dead?

I itch, therefore I am.

– But: might I be dead? Might I be unalive, might others be alive while I am not? Isn't this a variation on the anxiety about being asleep while others are awake, about missing the life that is happening while one is unable to observe or participate in it?

Notes towards a supreme itch. The son of an itch. The transcutaneous itch. Think about that or the pain, is there a none of the above? Bet that this leaking fluid would clean out one's insides, right enough, while it makes a mess of what's cheerily called the living room. None of the above.

– This transcutaneous itch, is it an illusion, and if so, what

141

evolutionary purpose does it serve?

Wait. Who said that?

– Or perhaps this question is actually a kind of answer. Sleeplessness as a natural de-selection, a kind of evolutionary suicide. The insomniacs on the march!

This heaving dance with the heavy device is no march. The lamp is all right, has steadied itself. Fluid all down the sleeve now, the lamp isn't impressed, but the lamp isn't thinking, it isn't. Open the drawer, of course it's stuck, as if on fucking cue. All for the love of thinking. The fluid's for drinking? The flood of thinking. Here's a spoon. Stop thinking, stop thinking, stop thinking. A thoughtless spoon. A spoon full of.

– All it takes.

How the most insignificant reflex is all it takes. A tightening or loosening of a muscle, if a supportive mechanism is brought into play, or in the case of ingesting some manner of toxic substance, just a few gulps. All of the words, the professed awareness and will, come down to just that, just a few gulps.

– Just a few gulps.

Is this me or is it. Push it, push it.

– Just a few gulps.

Push.

– Just a few gulps.

All right. Give it a rest.

# CAPTIVITY

When the rhino died, well.

    Are you sure this is...? Of interest...?

    You see, every day for nearly fourteen years she had walked to the zoo and visited the rhino. This did not involve talking to the rhino or anything like that: she never spoke to the animal, but stood or sat on nearby bench and watched the rhino, and was in turn observed by staff at the zoo, who recognized her as a regular but with whom she also did not speak. Some days she was there early in the morning, just after the zoo opened, some days she brought a modest lunch with her and ate it on the bench, and some days she came in the late afternoon. Apart from being daily the visits had no other apparent pattern.

    When the rhino died, she kept coming to the same spot, to the empty containment area, though she missed a day here or there, and when after a few months the containment area was refitted and given to the four ostriches...

It was sudden, certainly, but in another way it wasn't, you know. He had been weak and slowing down.

The eyes of the zookeepers, all of them, puffy for days.

A rhino, who's going to take that seriously, think that's. . .

Let's just call it a rhino. All right? It was a rhino.

Though what it is now, well.

Had there been more than one rhino, I know there wasn't, but had there been more than one, a bunch of them, do you know what that's called? A crash of rhinos. I shit you not. A crash of rhinos.

One young girl, she came to the zoo quite often, you know. She was terribly upset. She didn't say anything about it, but anyone could see.

Not that young. Not a girl. A young woman.

Not born in captivity, but found lost and young, its hornless mother awash with impatient flies a mile away. The rhino had come to this zoo and she had visited the very first week the rhino was there, and fell into her pattern shortly thereafter.

The rhino was a fixture for her, a staple of her routine, every morning and some days the modest lunch on the bench, and now her days have this gap, is all.

Romanticization isn't the word. Patronizing isn't the word. You assume that this woman has no other life, that her entire existence revolves around an animal in a cage, an animal she might never actually have noticed. Maybe she just liked sitting on that particular bench, maybe that particular bench had some sort of I don't know connection for her. Maybe she hated the rhino. Maybe wished it would die.

It did die. And it wasn't sudden.

Well, in a way. . .

The bench directly faced the rhino's cage. She used to sit right there and watch the rhino, every time she came. This is what you call observed data. The zookeepers are honest.

They call it a containment area.

What do they call a dead rhino? Maybe the technical term is dead rhino. No longer contained.

And this is. . .? Of interest, I mean?

Maybe she didn't need, doesn't need the rhino anymore. Maybe she has transcended the rhino, her need for the rhino, whatever it was. You probably never thought of that. Maybe the rhino was a temporary focus, a placeholder for something more real. Maybe the rhino only existed because she needed it to exist, and when she didn't need it any longer, well. Maybe and maybe and maybe. You probably never thought of any of this. You just see this young woman looking at a rhino. Unimaginative isn't the word.

Coccidioidomycosis. Say that thirty times. . .

Not everybody likes zoos. Not even the people who come to the zoos, even the regulars, would tell you that they like zoos as such. Only anecdotal data on that one.

To characterize the lunch as modest. . .

146

If you're going to feel bad for someone, why not feel bad for the four ostriches? They don't have any regular visitors. They just stand there, not being rhinos, having one another, eating the hats of children and whatever else. You might feel bad for the four ostriches.

If it's not about feeling bad, what is it about?

Yes, it's very interesting.

# DANCE MOVES OF THE NEAR FUTURE

## Looting

Grab, reach out and grab what you can, grab all of it. If everything must go, as much of it is going with you as you can manage, but don't be methodical, don't be selective, don't be calm. There may never be an opportunity like this again: the cameras are all off. If you don't take all of this merchandise, someone else will. Use your elbows to claim your grabbing space, thrust forward and back as you take hold here and pull, take hold there and pull. The goods come in all sizes. This is where delirium runs the show. You can move from spot to spot, but make it a running burst and not a light step or skip.

## Swarming

The honeybees are returned and you are the cause of their resurrection. They move with you. You are conjuring, and must give the swarms room to move around you, encircle you in a perpetually shifting and reforming embrace. No claps, no jerks, no stomps:

wide arm and leg movements. Be at one with the bees. Eventually lower yourself, liquidly. You, who have summoned them into being, gradually and wilfully become the honey they are making. You can dissolve into other dancers: individuality is gone. This is about the hive, the honey. This is sensual but should not be naughty. Be pure. Pure honey.

### Hopebringer

Your mother has just attempted suicide and after a day-long bus ride you have just arrived at the unfamiliar hospital where she is resting with a freshly pumped stomach. She is not sure where she is and tries not to tear up when she recalls this building from her youth. Tell her that she is alive, that she needs to stay alive, that you understand her desperation, yet that you are furious at her, that you are not furious at her, that your father should be here, that it is a good thing for him that your father is in fact not here, that she needs to stay alive, that she is alive, that you don't want this to happen again, please, no. Words will fail – you know they will – so come on, use your body!

*The Frisk (also called the Quake)*
Fact: the world didn't end when much of the American west coast sank into the ocean. Life carries on, and life is movement. The Quake music scene, based on the seismic recordings, makes that point abundantly clear. Your legs are long, long, long. You bestride the earth: no rising sea will claim you. Stop and cross your arms, Colossus: lean back a little and let everyone scope you out from below. There is no harm in sexing this one up a little, bringing in a little hip action, but keep that grandeur, that height.

*Singularity*
Begin with the derriere; or rather, let *it* begin with *you*. Watch your bottom shake of its own accord. Parts of you are awakening, discovering themselves. This is the new body politic, and it's natural to be fearful, even ultimately to panic. Any number of sequences can be tried, one part after the other, but it's too easy and often inelegant to awaken the hands too early, and of course the head is overtaken and swallowed up by the arms (and maybe, most dramatically, the legs, too) only at the close. The siege grows quickly but in necessary stages. Bumping into other dancers is fine but must be accidental; in fact, the accidentals are the essence of doing Singularity, which can go with even the most minimalist syncopation or bassline.

*The Malnutrition*
This one is pure sympathetic magic – it's all about the sympathy. Let the world see you know their hunger, how they transcend the hunger, how they refuse to be eaten by hunger. Eat the hunger, digest yourself, saying: there's more where that came from! Yes, I will have another! The mouth is naturally a big part of this one but it's not everything. Tight action, stay close to yourself. It's not about

flaunting. The world is poisoning you but you can take it. Wind down but do not collapse, do not flop. Refuse to be eaten.

### Lost in the Wood

Try not to show your fear. Try not to move, not even to shuffle your feet. Try not to lose body heat as the long night overcomes. Try not to see too clearly in the darkness. Try not to be seen. Try not to breathe loudly, if at all, if at all. Try to not to feel. Fail.

### Gelatinous Zooplankton

With the rise of the invertebrates, spinelessness has never been so hip. This dance, as many have observed, is a kind of variation on the earlier, somewhat shorter-lived Swarming. The club and the crowd and you must pulsate together. You are one of many, unable to stand, but together a triumphant, jellying wave. Be permeable, then permeate. Conquer the earth.

### Halcyon

Break the truce, tertiary arms, all of them, intrabonic pandiculation. Whoosh! Sacs filled. Extirpate. Don't harmonize oatic rheums. Coserge, semi-ulmaically, all available tethers, gnash, and again whooosh! Rinbock and randesmal. Thiff whall? Brow the last the wisma, brower the high the pelt. Sisters. Mind the sacs, rumminalama. Hasten wiced especially cold to the signal above. Rummina rumminalamalama. Tell us again.

# ACKNOWLEDGEMENTS

It's easy, in elegant diction,
To call it an innocent fiction,
But it comes in the same category
As a regular terrible story.

*The Pirates of Penzance*

Several of these regular terrible stories have previously appeared, sometimes in slightly different form, in the following journals: *BafterC, Bitterzoet Magazine, The Danforth Review, filling Station, Lowestoft Chronicle, Numéro Cinq, The Puritan, The Santa Monica Review,* and *Unlikely Stories.* My thanks to the respective editors.

A Writers' Work in Progress Grant from the Ontario Arts Council provided much-appreciated assistance for which I am grateful. My other great good luck has been with New Star Books: the enthusiasm, intelligence, and care that Rolf Maurer and Mike Leyne have brought to this book are of a rare and admirable degree.

It is good fortune to count shrewd readers among one's friends, and for their support, insights, and honesty, I am very thankful for Steve Beattie, Stephen Cain, Adam Dickinson, Gord Dueck, Monica Drenth, Douglas Glover, Steven Heighton, Jason Heroux, Gail and Julian Scala, and Emily Schultz. And saving the last dance for Clelia and Simone.